DANA MARTON
LAST SPY STANDING

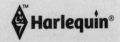

TORONTO NEW YORK LONDON
AMSTERDAM PARIS SYDNEY HAMBURG
STOCKHOLM ATHENS TOKYO MILAN MADRID
PRAGUE WARSAW BUDAPEST AUCKLAND

This book is dedicated to Karen Micek, a wonderful friend.
With many thanks to my editor, Allison Lyons.

Recycling programs
for this product may
not exist in your area.

ISBN-13: 978-0-373-74649-1

LAST SPY STANDING

Copyright © 2012 by Dana Marton

ABOUT THE AUTHOR

Dana Marton is the author of more than a dozen fast-paced, action-adventure romantic suspense novels and a winner of the Daphne du Maurier Award of Excellence. She loves writing books of international intrigue, filled with dangerous plots that try her tough-as-nails heroes and the special women they fall in love with. Her books have been published in seven languages in eleven countries around the world. When not writing or reading, she loves to browse antiques shops and enjoys working in her sizable flower garden, where she searches for "bad" bugs with the skills of a superspy and vanquishes them with the agility of a commando soldier. Every day in her garden is a thriller. To find more information on her books, please visit www.danamarton.com. She loves to hear from her readers and can be reached via email at DanaMarton@DanaMarton.com.

Books by Dana Marton

HARLEQUIN INTRIGUE

806—SHADOW SOLDIER
821—SECRET SOLDIER
859—THE SHEIK'S SAFETY
875—CAMOUFLAGE HEART
902—ROGUE SOLDIER
917—PROTECTIVE MEASURES
933—BRIDAL OP
962—UNDERCOVER SHEIK
985—SECRET CONTRACT*
991—IRONCLAD COVER*
1007—MY BODYGUARD*
1013—INTIMATE DETAILS*
1039—SHEIK SEDUCTION
1055—72 HOURS
1085—SHEIK PROTECTOR
1105—TALL, DARK AND LETHAL
1121—DESERT ICE DADDY
1136—SAVED BY THE MONARCH**
1142—ROYAL PROTOCOL**
1179—THE SOCIALITE AND THE BODYGUARD
1206—STRANDED WITH THE PRINCE**
1212—ROYAL CAPTIVE**
1235—THE SPY WHO SAVED CHRISTMAS
1299—THE BLACK SHEEP SHEIK
1328—LAST SPY STANDING

*Mission: Redemption
**Defending the Crown

CAST OF CHARACTERS

Megan Cassidy—She is full of secrets and on a desperate mission in the South American jungle. This is difficult enough without making a formidable enemy in Mitch Mendoza, a no-nonsense undercover operative who awakens impossible needs in her.

Mitch Mendoza—Member of a top-secret military group (SDDU). He is on a rescue op, his only goal being to find his target and take the man home. But everything gets a lot more complicated when a sexy, mysterious woman shows up in the middle of the jungle and stands in his way.

Zak Goodman—The son of the governor of Kansas, Zak chose a different path than his father. When he's involved in a drug deal gone bad, he finds himself the prisoner of a powerful drug lord south of the border

Juarez—A powerful drug captain, he controls a large chunk of the jungle.

Don Pedro—He's the top boss of the drug business in the region, with several captains reporting to him. They fear and loathe him at the same time. With good reason.

SDDU—Special Designation Defense Unit. A top-secret military team established to fight terrorism and other international crime that affects the U.S. Its existence is known only by a select few. Members are recruited from the best of the best.

Colonel Wilson—Mitch's boss. He's the leader of the SDDU, reporting straight to the Homeland Security Secretary.

Chapter One

The unforgiving South American sun scorched Mitch Mendoza's neck as he watched three men on the hillside below him through a pair of high-powered binoculars.

His current mission had only two rules. *Rule number one:* Don't mess up. *Rule number two:* If you mess up, don't leave witnesses.

The three men, aka the witnesses he wasn't supposed to leave, moved at a good clip. They were local, used to the jungle terrain and the humidity that made breathing difficult for outsiders who had no business being in these parts. Outsiders like Zak "Kid Kansas" Goodman who gasped for breath as he tried to keep up with Mitch.

"We can't let them reach the river." Mitch let the binoculars drop against his chest and looked back at the twenty-two-year-old trust-fund jerk whose only ambition seemed to be finding trouble and annoying as many people as possible in the process.

The boy was a long way from his fancy college fraternity, scratched and gaunt, wearing the signs of his recent imprisonment. "They're just a couple of goatherds. Let them be."

Mitch didn't think the kid had developed a conscience—although, that would have been nice. More likely, he was just too lazy to pick up the pace, too soft to put in the effort that would be necessary to catch up.

"I'm hungry. I want a break." He was worse than a three-year-old whining, *Are we there yet?* from the backseat.

"Soon." Mitch moved forward, adjusting his half empty backpack.

Their food had run out the day before. Neither of them had washed since last Friday. Not that he would have said they were roughing it. They still had a bottle of drinking water between them, and a tent to keep out the poisonous creepy crawlers that liked to pay jungle trekkers nighttime visits.

"Watch your step."

The faster they went, the more careful they had to be. Snakes hid in the undergrowth, stones blocked their steps on the uneven ground. Neither of them could afford a twisted ankle. They needed to catch up with those goatherds. Quickly.

Word that two Americans were trespassing through infamous drug kingpin Juarez's part of the jungle could not reach the nearest village. Or the head of the local *polizia*. If the police chief was corrupt, he'd report right back to Juarez. If he was clean, he'd report the info to his superiors. Mitch didn't need complications like that. Enough had gone wrong already.

The trip should have been a simple in-and-out rescue op, except that Zak wasn't the clueless victim his file had indicated. Mitch had found him in a shed on Juarez property just as the kid had shot the drug lord's second in command. Juarez's brother-in-law, in fact.

That wasn't going to be forgiven.

Juarez was going to move heaven and earth to find the idiot. What had the kid been thinking anyway? He'd shoot his way out of camp and make it out of the jungle? He would have been dead within the hour if Mitch hadn't been watching the camp for days; if he hadn't been ready to grab the kid and run with him.

He pushed forward and knew without

having to turn around that Zak was falling behind. The kid made a lot of noise.

"Keep up and keep quiet." His mission was to get Kid Kansas, aka Kansas Governor Conrad Goodman's son, out of the South American jungle in one piece without anyone knowing that he'd been there in the first place.

They didn't exactly have authorization from the local government. Mitch didn't have authorization from his own government, for that matter. Just a request from Colonel Wilson. The governor and the Colonel went way back, to a double tour of duty in 'Nam. They were blood brothers.

That the Colonel trusted Mitch with the mission was an honor. Mitch would have walked through fire for the man.

He looked up at the sun and prayed for a little luck, although he was used to his prayers going unanswered. But maybe this was his lucky day, because suddenly the three men he was following stopped. It looked like they were going to have a bite before crossing the river.

"Let's move." He set the pace even faster.

"I can't."

"Should have stayed home, then."

"It's not my fault I was kidnapped," the kid snapped. He was getting his spirit back and then some.

Right after he'd shot Juarez's brother-in-law, he'd been ready to fall apart, panicking when Mitch had busted into his prison. But in the past two days, once he'd realized his escape had been successful, he'd come to consider himself some sort of an action hero—or, at the very least, Mitch's equal.

"I don't deserve any of this," the boy kept on whining.

"You didn't come to Bogota for sightseeing."

The governor had bought that line from his spoiled son. Mitch didn't. But Zak's lies were an issue for another day. Right now, he had bigger fish to fry. The men in front of them weren't his only problem. Juarez's soldiers were hunting for Zak, and they couldn't be far behind.

He got the kid down the hill in twenty minutes, stashed him in some nearby bushes, then moved toward the men's camp. The goatherds had already lit a fire to warm water for their *yerba maté,* a favorite herbal drink of most South American natives.

They seemed simple men, each traveling

with a single bag, wearing worn, mismatched clothes under their equally tattered ponchos. Their only crime had been being at the wrong place at the wrong time. Then again, better men than these had been killed for lesser reasons. And how many truly innocent men hung out in this part of the jungle? Where was their herd, for starters?

What had they been doing that close to Juarez's camp? The day after Mitch had rescued Zak, he'd stashed him out of harm's way and left the idiot for half an hour, so he could double back and see how close their pursuers were getting. Zak's only job had been to sit tight. But when he'd heard people moving through the woods, he lost his head and panicked. He'd run, yelling for Mitch in English. The goatherds had seen him.

And for that, they would have to die. Mitch checked his gun with distaste. He didn't condone senseless killing. And he hated having his hand forced by Zak, who should have simply followed him out of the jungle, quietly appreciating the rescue along the way.

He shook all that off and focused on what he was about to do. He would take these men out because he had to. But he wasn't going to shoot them in the back. He took a deep breath and stepped out into the clearing.

The next second, ponchos were shoved aside, the men—definitely not simple goatherds—aiming AK-47s at him. Mitch's index finger curled around the trigger of his weapon, adrenaline shooting into his bloodstream.

But instead of all hell breaking loose, everything became absurdly surreal as a blonde suburban housewife stepped out of the bushes at the edge of the clearing. She wore khaki capri pants and a matching tank top, blond waves tumbling around her heart-shaped face, translucent amber eyes as wide as they could be. She looked like she came straight from a backyard barbecue or a kid's birthday party. The only things missing were the oven mitts.

"Excuse me. I'm sorry. Can you help me?"

Then their moment of grace was over and the "goatherds" opened fire on Mitch. They apparently didn't consider the woman much of a threat. Mitch dove for the bushes to avoid the flying bullets. But one nicked him in the shoulder. He ignored the burn as he shot and rolled, careful to avoid Blondie.

Lucky for her, he was good at what he did. The fight ended in seconds.

She stood in the same spot, her feet frozen to the ground, her entire body trembling. And he noticed now that her clothes were stained in places, her hands dirty.

"Oh," she said, as he came to his feet, blood trickling down his arm. Her full lips trembled faintly. "I think I'm going to be sick."

"Don't move." He patted her down, feeling surprised, and a little guilty, that he enjoyed it. Her eyes went even wider, and her cheeks blushed pink.

When he was done, he slipped the small designer backpack off her shoulders and checked over the contents: a small first aid kit, bug spray, suntan lotion, extra clothes and a water bottle with a filter that made even mud puddles safe to drink. No weapons.

He gave the bag back. Damned if he knew what to make of her. "Okay. Get sick if you need to."

She ran for the bushes she'd come from, and a second later he could hear her retching.

He turned to the bodies on the sand, then to Zak, who was inching forward from his hiding spot. He looked green around the gills, too. He threw a questioning look toward the bushes where they could still hear their mysterious guest.

Mitch shrugged and collected the weapons. "Go see what they have in their bags." Food would be welcome. He looked with regret at the *yerba maté* that had been spilled.

"Hey, check this out!" Zak held up two-kilo bags of white powder a minute later, grinning from ear to ear.

Mitch leveled his gaze on the idiot. "Rip it open, then dump it into the river."

"What? No way."

Mitch went stock-still. "Dump it into the river or I'll leave you here to rot."

A long minute passed before the kid sprinkled the white powder over the water, his stance belligerent. He took a quick sniff from the back of his hand when he thought Mitch wasn't looking.

The governor of Kansas was a decent man, but too softhearted. He was going to have to learn tough love in a hurry if he wanted to straighten out his son. Mitch didn't envy him.

He collected the AK-47s and tossed them into the river. He had plenty of ammo for his own gun and didn't need the extra weight to carry in this heat. No way he was giving one to the kid.

The bushes rustled as Blondie returned, none too steady on her feet. She kept her distance. She was too pretty to look truly pitiful, but she looked tussled—in a curvaceous, wholesome way. "Are you Americans?"

She wasn't the kind of woman Mitch could relate to. He didn't exactly lead a suburban lifestyle. He fixed Zak with a look to keep him quiet. "Who are you and what are you doing here?"

"Megan Cassidy. From New Jersey. I'm on a South American orchid tour." She swallowed hard. "We were attacked in the jungle."

Here? What was she on, the kamikaze boat run by Stupid Tours? He swatted some bugs away. "How many people?"

"Twenty-two of us tourists..." Her voice faltered. "Plus the two guides."

He felt infinitely tired all of a sudden. He didn't have time to rush into the jungle. He couldn't. It wasn't part of his mission. He asked anyway. "Survivors?"

"Just me." Tears spilled over and ran down her alabaster skin.

He didn't trust tears. He never knew when they were genuine and when they were used to simply manipulate a man. Her crying made him uneasy.

What did people like her think they were doing in the jungle? Hell, she shouldn't have been allowed in the country. Women like her should stick to attending PTA meetings, sipping double lattes while strolling through the mall and playing golf at the country club.

"I need to go home." She swallowed a sob. "Could you help me find the nearest town? I need to get to the police and an airport. Please?"

An unwanted complication at a time when he couldn't afford to be slowed down. "When did all this happen?"

She blinked rapidly. "This morning."

"How far away?"

"I don't know." She sniffed. "I kept running."

He hadn't heard gunshots, but the dense greenery muffled sound—the jungle formed solid walls in places. It all came down to this: he had no way of figuring out where exactly the massacre had taken place. And he had no time to look for it.

He finished considering his options, and shot Zak a look to remind him to keep quiet. "I'm Mitch and this is Zak here. From

Panama. We're hiking buddies. Just got on this trail when these drug runners ambushed us," he lied with practiced ease.

He didn't want to have to kill her, and didn't have the heart to leave her, either. But he would, if she became a threat to his mission. "About that attack on your group…"

She folded her arms around her slim midriff, her skin tightening over her cheekbones. "Would you mind if we didn't talk about it? Just right now, I mean?" Her amber eyes begged him. There went those trembling lips again.

The sight of her twisted something in the middle of his chest, an unfamiliar sensation he didn't care for. He supposed his questions could wait. "You can come with us as far as the nearest town."

She looked ready to melt with relief. "Thank you. I won't be any trouble, I swear."

He didn't believe that for a second.

Her shoulders straightened as she visibly pulled herself together. "What can I do to help?"

All right, she got a point for that. He'd yet to hear that question from Zak.

"Take whatever food and water you can find and store it in our backpacks," he told her. He nodded at Zak to help her, then went to see about the bodies.

He searched their clothes, but found little beyond cigarettes. No ID on any of them. The last thing people like this would have wanted, if they were caught, was for the *polizia* to be able to identify them.

Ten minutes later, the current carried the bodies of the three goatherds-slash-drug runners downriver. Another minute and the bags were packed. Mitch's had been hit, his GPS/radio unit among the casualties. It would have been a lot worse if he'd lost that on his way in. But from this point on, the way back out was fairly straightforward.

As he swung his backpack over his shoulder, he caught Megan looking at him.

"Let me see to your wound." She stepped closer, her movements hesitant, but her gaze determined.

His shoulder. Back at home, he would have ignored something this small, but it wouldn't be smart to risk an infection in the jungle.

"All right." But he watched her carefully. She hadn't taken the earlier gunfight well. He didn't want her to faint at the sight of his blood.

She seemed more together now as she

peeled back the torn fabric of his shirt, took a good look, then went for her first aid kit.

Zak wiggled his eyebrows at Mitch from behind her. He glared back at the kid who seemed to have little on his brain beyond drugs and women. He looked decidedly less tired than he had before Megan showed up. His gaze kept returning to her, lingering on her curves.

"Try to focus on something useful," Mitch told him. "It tends to increase the chances of survival in a place like this."

He rolled his eyes, but asked, "Where do we cross?"

"I'll figure that out. Don't you worry."

The woman's glance darted to the river, concern in her eyes, before she returned her attention to the task at hand, her movements quick and efficient. He wouldn't even have felt her light touch as she cleaned and bandaged his wound if he wasn't so damned aware of her. He closed his eyes so at least he wouldn't have to watch those long, slim fingers as they touched his skin.

He stepped back the second she finished. "Thanks."

She couldn't have been much older than the kid was. No more than late twenties. In some ways, he felt ancient compared to the two of them. A couple of years of black ops duty had a way of aging a person. But not enough, it seemed. He definitely wasn't too old to appreciate the way she moved. He caught himself. He wasn't any better than Kid Idiot, the two of them ogling her as she packed away her emergency kit.

He cleared his throat and glanced up and down the river, evaluating the height of the opposite bank and the speed of the current. "We'll cross right here," he decided after a moment of deliberation.

If the locals had picked this spot, it had to be the easiest crossing in the vicinity. He looked back at the jungle behind them, watching closely for a few seconds. Listening did no good—the noise of the river blocked any distant sounds. He didn't see any flocks of birds suddenly taking flight or movement in the vegetation. That didn't guarantee anything, but he'd learned over the years to trust his instincts. He felt reasonably sure that Juarez's men hadn't caught up with them yet. Crossing the river should be safe, as long as they didn't stay out in the open longer than was absolutely necessary.

"Let's go." He reached for the woman's

small hand and nodded for Zak to take the other one. They strode into the water, the three of them forming a human chain.

"If we get separated and washed down-river, turn on your back and aim your body toward the other shore at an angle. Don't fight the current. Work with it." He had to raise his voice to be heard over the rushing of the river now that they were standing in the shallows.

The water wasn't high, but it moved fast in its narrow bed. Which was better than slow water and the pools it formed. At least, here they didn't have to worry about piranhas, poisonous water snakes or alligators. All they had to contend with was the current and any logs that might wash along under the water. Being hit by one of those wouldn't be pleasant. He knew from experience.

Soon they were in up to their knees and Mitch fought to keep his balance. "Remember, if the water breaks you loose, stay on your back."

"Why?" Megan had his hand in a death grip, her delicate fingers folded tightly around his.

"To protect your vital organs. There might be sharp rocks on the river bottom, or logs and other junk being swept along under the surface."

She paled.

"You'll be fine." He was trying to find the right words to reassure someone like her, but came up empty. He felt like he should carry her out of the jungle without letting any danger touch her. He felt guilty that he couldn't, then angry at himself for feeling guilty. He hadn't asked for any of this.

He couldn't let her mess with his head. He had no time to mollycoddle her. He swore under his breath. She was definitely going to slow them down, despite her promises.

But she did keep up in the water. He didn't have to drag her or anything. She did slip once, but he was quick to haul her up against him.

Wet top. Award-winning curves. Man, it'd been a long time since…

He made himself look away.

Zak's eyes were seven kinds of shiny and glued to her. Mitch frowned at the kid and kept going, testing the river bottom with his foot at each step before putting his weight on it.

In the end, he was the one who messed up. When she slipped again and this time went under, he was suddenly all thumbs, not wanting to grab anything, um, delicate. A moment of hesitation, but it cost him. As she scrambled to right herself, her frenetically moving legs kicked his legs right out from under him.

Zak pulled her up. Mitch let go of her, not wanting to pull her back down with him. He tried to stand, but finding purchase on the muddy bottom was no easy task. His feet couldn't find purchase on the slippery silt.

The current carried him downriver.

"Get to shore. I'll find you," he shouted back to them, trying not to swallow too much of the frothy water.

Zak looked green with panic. She didn't. Probably because she didn't know enough to realize how much trouble they were in, two complete amateurs in the middle of a raging river.

Chapter Two

An eternity seemed to pass before Mitch crawled up the muddy bank on the other side of the river, exhausted from battling the current. He scanned the hillside behind him.

No sign of Juarez's men. Yet.

He could see Megan helping Zak out of the water a few hundred feet away. She hadn't panicked. In fact, she had enough presence of mind to even help the kid. *Maybe she isn't as helpless as she looks,* he thought as he began marching toward them.

"Better get into the woods and out of this sun." He took charge when he reached them, leading them into the cover of the trees so they wouldn't be seen from the other side. They could use some rest, and this place was as good as any.

On closer inspection, she did look shaken. And more than a little lost. She kept casting worried looks at him. He couldn't blame her.

This morning she'd been on a bus tour that she'd thought was safe. She had no way of knowing that the only roads up here were the ones cut into the jungle by loggers who were little more than criminals, clearing the jungle illegally. Traversing those roads without permission from the local crime lord could be deadly. Without protection, the bandits who controlled the area would consider anyone on them free prey.

Whoever had put her tour together was running an irresponsible operation, exploiting tourists who didn't know better. He'd probably figured he could take a few people in and out quickly, without being seen. Idiot.

And so were the people who would sign up for a trip like this. You couldn't hire the first local guide that showed up at your hotel. Nor should you get on the first rickety bus that promised a grand adventure. He had half a mind to tell her that, but she looked like she'd already paid plenty for her error in judgment. She'd almost paid with her life. The thought set his teeth on edge.

"What did your husband have to say about you coming all this way for a flower?" he asked once they were settled on a big rock, shaking water out of their boots. He wanted to know what kind of man would let a delicate woman like her come to a dangerous place like this.

"I'm not married." She finger combed her hair, then pulled her clothes away from her skin. She seemed to be trying to air-dry the fabric, but it wasn't going to happen anytime soon considering the humidity level.

He tried not to look much, but it wasn't easy. She had perfect proportions. Everywhere. And a pretty face, with symmetrical features, thick lashes and full lips. She radiated a kind of wholesome innocence he didn't know what to do with.

He took the cheese and chunk of flatbread that they'd taken from the goatherds out of his waterproof backpack, and divided the food between Zak and Megan. "You go ahead. I'm not hungry."

He'd eat grubs if he got desperate. He had a feeling the other two wouldn't.

"You two hike a lot in these parts?" she asked between two bites.

"Here and in other places." His missions took him all over the world.

As far as the kid went, this was Zak's first trip to South America. Based on the scant information he'd been given, Mitch knew Zak had graduated from being a pothead to more serious vices and decided that as long as he was using, he might as well get into the business. He'd probably taken one too many college business classes and fancied himself an entrepreneur. And since he learned from his father that when you wanted to get something done, you went to the top, he bought a ticket to South America.

Big mistake.

"How far is the nearest town?" Megan wiggled her toes in the sunshine. They were tipped with nail polish and looked like candy. Her pants were rolled up to above her knees.

He looked away. Her dainty toes and long legs were none of his business. "We should be there by nightfall."

"Do they have an airport?"

Sure. Right next to the day spa. "We'll be lucky to find a phone and a shack to sleep in. We're in a sparsely populated area. There isn't any industry around here, and little agriculture. The natives farm a little, but mostly they live off the jungle's bounty." He didn't mention the criminal element, didn't want to remind her.

In the morning, he would hook her up with a dependable guide who'd take her to the nearest city. She couldn't come with them any farther. When he contacted the Colonel, they'd get a military transport out of the country, which wasn't something she could be allowed to see.

"But they have shops, right?" She tugged on her top, her eyes filled with embarrassment. "This outfit is completely ruined. Everything else I have is soaking wet from the river, too."

Educating her on the local realities didn't seem worth the energy. She'd be out of his hair tomorrow morning. Simpler for him and safer for her. She was a babe in the woods. Megan Cassidy had no business being someplace like this, around men like him.

THEY REACHED THE TOWN at twilight, walking out of the rain forest tired and dirty.

Mitch wiped the sweat off his forehead as he led his small team toward the largest wooden building he could see. Kids ran around in the dust, chasing dogs and small, black pigs. The hum of generators filled the air, providing the few dozen houses with electricity. A couple of ancient bicycles leaned against crumbling walls. A beat-up, rusted-out pickup—probably the only car in the village—hid in the shade of a fruit tree.

He scanned the scene before him carefully, but everything seemed as it should be. He couldn't spot anyone paying them undue attention. Juarez's influence may or may not extend as far as this place. But even if Juarez *was* looking this far afield, he'd have people watching for a young man, not two men and a woman. They had that going for them, a definite advantage.

"Hola!" They reached the building, and he slowly pushed the door in.

The local guesthouse had four rooms, the toothless old man who shuffled out from the back explained, but one had burned out and two were permanently occupied, so only one was free. He didn't have a phone, but there was one in the next village, fifty kilometers to the east. Mitch paid in advance, took the key, then led the others down the hallway to the room the man indicated.

"This is it." The door stood ajar. He nudged it open with his boot, his hand near his weapon, ready for ambush, ready for anything. Juarez's men could have cut in front of them.

But as he looked around, it didn't seem they did. Nobody waited for them in there save a handful of cockroaches that skittered across the floor. A single bed took up most of the room, covered by a torn blanket that might have had bright-colored stripes at one point in the distant past, but was now beyond faded.

He could hear Megan swallowing behind him.

"Didn't the sign on the front say *LUJO?* Doesn't that mean luxury in Spanish?" Her voice was a touch faint.

He felt sorry for her. She was so far out of her element… "We have our own bathroom. And you'll be in a nice hotel by tomorrow this time. Hang in there just a little longer."

She nodded bravely.

He walked forward to the open door in the corner, and took in the small shower that probably had only cold water. The chipped toilet had no seat. The pipes were rusty, but none of them were leaking. And he didn't have to worry about water quality as long as they had their filter bottles.

Not that Megan appreciated their good fortune—having a roof over their heads and all. Her eyes were unnaturally wide and brimming with something that looked suspiciously close to tears. Even Zak was looking around with a dubious expression on his face.

He couldn't allow them to fall apart now. "Sit."

They both obeyed.

"This is what we're going to do. We'll clean up then have a decent meal. Then we'll get some rest." He looked at Megan. "You should wait to report the attack until you reach a bigger place. The *polizia* in a village like this is probably one man. He won't be able to do much. And he might even be in league with the bandits."

Plus, he didn't want any part of the police report. If they were together when she went to the authorities, the police would also want to talk to him and Zak.

She went a shade paler, probably remembering the attack, but she nodded.

He couldn't let her think too much. "All right. Let's get on with the cleaning up. I don't know about you, but I'm pretty hungry. The sooner we get ourselves in decent enough shape to go out and look for food, the better."

Zak went first. He didn't take long, then settled in front of an ancient radio bolted to the wall, trying to make it work while Megan took her turn. She didn't loiter, either, confirming Mitch's suspicions about the water being unheated. He was about to ask Zak, but then the bathroom door opened and she stood there wrapped in nothing but a worn towel.

His tongue got stuck to the roof of his mouth.

She had legs a mile long. Lean, pink thighs. Zak stared at her wide-eyed, with a stupid grin on his face. She tugged the towel down in a self-conscious gesture that nearly caused her breasts to spill out on top. She looked desperate and embarrassed, the hottest thing Mitch had seen in years. Or ever.

Stop staring, get moving, he told himself, and after a few seconds he actually did it.

He moved to grab his gun off the dresser, but she moved toward her bag on the bed at the same time, getting between him and his weapon.

In nothing but a towel.

Which would have been just fine—more than fine—if she were a different sort of woman, if they were alone and he wasn't in the middle of a clandestine mission.

He practically ran for the bathroom, needing that cold shower ASAP.

"I'll be out in a minute," he called through the closed door, wiping the sweat from his forehead.

He peeled off his clothes, stepped into the

shower and let the cold spray hit his head. Exactly what he needed. He tried not to think of Megan Cassidy in that flimsy towel, those legs or those wet, soft locks framing her delicate face.

Morning couldn't come too quickly. She needed to get far away from places like this and men like him.

He quieted the little voice in his head that said he should put Zak on the military transport then stay behind and personally escort Miss Cassidy back home to make sure nothing bad happened to her.

That voice had nothing to do with her long, lean thighs. Rescue missions just ran deep in his blood. He couldn't help it if his instincts were to rescue her, too.

She was the proverbial damsel in distress, a scared, lost little thing who'd gone through considerable trauma in the past day. She collected orchids in New Jersey. This was probably the first massacre she'd ever seen.

He couldn't relate to a life that sheltered.

He was drying off when he heard a crash come from the bedroom. He didn't stop to dress, just burst through the door without thought, ready for fighting. He swore viciously at the sight that greeted him.

Zak was tied up on the bed, a rag in his mouth keeping him quiet. Megan stood in the middle of the room, dressed in shorts and a black tank top, boots on, hair pulled back into a no-nonsense ponytail, looking like the lead character in a kick-butt video game. A fierce scar ran from her ear to her throat, a pink line her tumbling locks had covered up until now.

All uncertainty was gone from her fiery amber eyes, all paleness gone from her face as she glared at Mitch and pointed his own gun at him. She held a matching weapon in her other hand.

Where did she get that from? "Put them down," he ordered.

Instead, she stepped closer.

"Who are you?"

"Who are *you?*" She turned the question on him. "Definitely not a hiker from Panama." She shoved one weapon into the back of her waistband, pulled a plastic cuff from her back pocket—one she had to have stolen from his backpack—then gestured toward the water pipes in the bathroom behind him.

"No." He measured the distance between them, judging it too great to be covered in a single leap. He was going for it anyway.

Or not.

She squeezed off a shot that passed so close to his ear he could feel the wind of the bullet.

"Hey, all right." He stepped back, knowing no help would be coming. In a place like this, people knew enough to walk away from gunfire, not toward it.

She tossed him the plastic tie. "The pipe."

He took a step back, held his left hand up to the pipe and cuffed himself to it. He swore under his breath, not taking his eyes off her for a second. He'd been had. He couldn't remember the last time that had happened.

What in hell had he been thinking? But of course, he hadn't been thinking at all. She'd short-circuited his brain the moment she'd stepped into that clearing.

He flashed her his most lethal glare. "The money I have on me ain't worth it, honey. I'm going to track you down. That's a promise."

She gave him a cocky smile, keeping her gaze above his shoulders, then turned away, leaving him handcuffed and naked.

But if he thought this was about cash, he realized his mistake a second later when she untied Zak roughly and yanked him to his feet, not paying any attention to the boy's muffled groaning.

"You let him be," Mitch ordered on a voice that usually brought results.

She didn't even bother with a backward glance as she shoved Zak out the door. The next thing Mitch heard was the door slamming behind them and the key turning.

The sound of a car's motor coming to life reached his ears a minute later, as he desperately searched the bathroom for a tool that could set him free. Under his breath, he cursed Megan Cassidy—if that was her real name—a hundred different ways, each singularly inventive.

Chapter Three

The rumble of the ancient motor drowned out the sounds of the rain forest, but not the strange noises the kid made behind the gag.

"Are you going to keep quiet if I take it off?" Megan glanced over as she drove the geriatric pickup down an uneven dirt road that cut through the jungle.

Zak glared at her and sounded as if he were trying to swear around the cloth.

"Then I'm sorry, but you're going to stay this way." Not that she enjoyed making anyone uncomfortable on purpose.

But he could breathe. She was going to save herself from having to listen to more of the threats and the names he'd called her when she'd tried to take out the gag the first time. She wasn't going to put up with that from some two-bit drug dealer who got on Juarez's bad side.

She didn't know who he was and she didn't

care. All she cared about was returning him to the boss and getting that next promotion, the next level of trust that would allow her to accompany Juarez to the meeting at Don Pedro's hidden stronghold next week.

The logging road she was on was about to end, which meant they would have to hoof it thirty miles south to the next passable road she knew, the one she'd left her ATV on before she cut through the jungle to cut off the kid at the river. She had figured that would be the way he would go if he knew anything.

Unfortunately, she hadn't found him alone, which had required some quick thinking and cost her a lot of wasted time. Mitch was... Never mind that. She didn't have all the details and she didn't need them, not even if he had the most amazing body she'd ever seen and the most dangerous bedroom eyes she could imagine. Juarez's orders were only for the kid.

She drove to the point where the jungle became impassable, left the pickup and shoved Zak forward on the foot trail ahead. His head was red with fury as he dragged his feet.

She shoved him harder. "I'd prefer if you

walked. It's easier than dragging a dead body over terrain like this. Of course, the boss probably wouldn't want the whole body."

She pretended to ponder the point then put a smile on her face. "As long as I take some vital organ that proves you're dead, it should be enough for him."

The kid's eyes went wide. He picked up the pace.

She undid the snaps at her hips and rolled down her pant legs, transforming her shorts to long cargo pants, the bottom of which she tucked into her boots to keep herself safe from bugs and scratches. Then she pulled a light shirt from her backpack, completing her preparations for the jungle. And she did it all on the go, without missing a step.

She kept an eye on their surroundings as they pushed ahead, looking for anything edible, alert to possible danger. "Watch for snakes on or near the trail. And poison frogs."

Her stomach growled for the meal they'd missed at that guesthouse. The small chunk of bread and goat cheese they'd eaten after crossing the river hadn't been nearly enough. But she didn't have time to leave the trail and forage right now. Night would be falling soon, and before that happened, she had to find a place to camp and make a platform that would keep them off the ground while they slept.

Even a raised bed didn't guarantee that they wouldn't awake with a snake or a tarantula up their pant leg, but at least it would improve the odds in their favor. Regardless of what she'd threatened the kid with, she intended to take him back to Juarez alive and in one piece.

Which meant they were going to sit the night out. Walking through the jungle after dark was suicide. She wasn't foolish enough to attempt that. And they both needed rest, anyway. You got tired, you made mistakes. Then you were no help to anyone.

They walked an hour before she found a good spot, a clearing with bamboo nearby and big-leaf palms that had gathered rainwater she could collect in her safe-filter water bottle. She'd forgotten to fill it at the guesthouse. Okay, not forgotten. But once Mitch had been cuffed to the pipes, it hadn't seemed too smart to go near the sink.

She wasn't going to think of the way she'd left him. Naked.

She'd almost dropped her guns when he'd

busted out of that bathroom, all muscles and tanned skin.

"Here." She hung her backpack on a branch and used her short machete to cut enough bamboo for a double bed and enough vines to suspend it. When she was done, she pulled the rag from Zak's mouth.

"Keep quiet," she ordered before she showed him what she wanted him to do. "I'd recommend you do a good job. You don't want to sleep on the ground here, believe me."

She wasn't a great fan of the jungle. The past year hadn't been fun, exactly. But she would have put up with worse to achieve her aim. She scanned the trees and moved toward one that seemed to have potential, all while trying not to think of Mitch—and failing.

"Where are you taking me?" Zak called after her. Dirty and exhausted, he sounded a lot more subdued than when he'd screamed choice obscenities at her earlier.

She ignored that question as she got working on the bay leaf palms locals used for thatching to keep the rain out of their huts. "We need a roof to keep us dry overnight."

"Why does it rain so much here?" he whined,

pulling his shirt away from his neck where the wet clothing had rubbed the skin raw.

She had some salve that would work on that.

"Because it's a rain forest." She kept Zak in sight as she worked. When she dragged the palm fronds back, she helped him finish the beds—he hadn't gotten far—then put the roof on, thatching it as best she could. The sky was already darkening by the time she finished. They had only minutes to start a fire.

She grabbed a dry cotton sock from her backpack and used that as kindling, wondering how far Mitch was behind them. Far enough, hopefully. She hadn't seen another vehicle at the village.

Getting a fire going in a place that dripped with moisture was quite the trick, but the burning sock dried the bamboo shavings she piled on, and then that caught fire at last. Just in time. The jungle around them was already black. Because of the tall trees, night here was a sudden thing. You'd better hope you were ready for it.

"Here, put this on your neck." She tossed the small jar of salve to the kid, then tied his left foot to the platform with some vines and one quick hook.

"You can't do that to me!" He yanked his bonds, his face turning red with outrage. "What if some wild animal attacks us? How do I escape?"

She put more wood on the fire then climbed onto her side of the platform, stashing the guns so they were at hand for her but out of reach for the kid. "If any trouble comes our way, I'll take care of it."

He swore viciously, but did it under his breath this time. And he didn't try to attack her, mindful of her weapons. Good. He wasn't an all-around idiot then. He seemed to have the ability to learn.

"Where are you taking me?" he asked again.

"Back to the camp."

"I have money—my father has money—"

She needed sleep. "No." However much drug money the kid and his family had, there weren't enough greenbacks in the world to tempt her. Something a lot more important was at stake.

Zak fell into sullen silence. Bugs began their night serenade. A macaw cried somewhere above them in the canopy.

She closed her eyes, ignoring her growling stomach. In the morning, as soon as there was sufficient light, she would find something to eat.

Her dreams were jumbled, and mostly involved Mitch. In some of the dreams, he was naked in her bed. In others, he was trying to kill her.

She woke in the dead of the night to a noise that didn't fit in with the rest of the sounds of the jungle. Or had she dreamed it? She listened carefully. No. Even the insect chorus was off. Something was disturbing their nightly routine.

Their fire had burned down to embers, providing little visibility. She reached for her weapon as quietly as possible and waited.

SHE WAS AWAKE but she hadn't seen him yet. Mitch crouched in the cover of some bamboo. The smartest thing would be to shoot her right now, but he wanted to know who she was and who she worked for. She intrigued him, he couldn't deny that. It kept her alive. For now.

"Drop both guns to the ground," he told her without showing himself.

After a moment of hesitation, she did, then slipped from her shelter, searching the darkness in the direction of his voice. "How did you find us?"

He'd followed the logging road on the *polizia* man's motorbike, then tracked their trail through the jungle. "I could smell the smoke of your fire from miles away."

"I didn't think you'd be so close behind," she admitted, then pulled a machete from behind her back and came at him.

How in hell did she see him?

The first blow almost took off his nose. He dropped the old pistol he'd bought in the village, knowing he wasn't going to use it, not yet, not until he had some answers. And for that, he needed both hands to restrain her.

He grabbed her wrist and held the machete away from them. She launched herself at him again, and they ended up grappling on the ground in short order, which was a really bad idea, considering all the poisonous bugs and snakes. The sooner he got her under control the better.

"Quit it," he snapped at her.

She ignored him.

He kicked the embers as they rolled, and the flames livened up, giving them both a little more light. He could see Zak from the corner of his eye, working madly on the restraint on his leg.

"You stay where you are," he growled at

the kid. The last thing he needed was for the idiot to pick up one of the discarded guns and shoot him by accident.

That small diversion—his attention on Zak for a split second—was enough for her to make her move. She flawlessly executed a flip he remembered from special ops training. *Interesting.* And where would she have learned that?

He responded with a move a martial arts fanatic taught him while he'd spent two years deep undercover in Thailand. That made her eyes go wide and got him control of the machete at last.

He tossed the weapon aside and pinned her to the ground, embarrassed to be breathing so hard. Her firm breasts pressed into his chest. That image of her at the guesthouse, wearing nothing but a towel, popped into his mind. He batted it away. "Where did you get your training?"

"Where did you get yours?" She strained against him, taxing his focus.

"Who do you work for?" *Don't think lean pink thighs.*

"Same guy everyone works for around here." She grunted with frustration as she tried to heave him off, undaunted by the sixty or so pounds he had on her.

He kept her firmly in place, ignoring the interesting ways her body moved under his. At another time, in another place... *Focus*. "Not me."

"Let me guess, you're Cristobal's."

Cristobal was a rival drug lord, controlling vast territories north of the river. He had the reputation of being a ruthless bastard who didn't hesitate to burn whole villages if someone crossed him.

"Guess again." He transferred both of her wrists to one hand, then reached out with the other and grabbed his gun from the ground, feeling much better with a weapon handy.

She stared at the barrel and turned all soft under him, her large eyes filling with tears. "Juarez is going to kill me if I don't bring the kid back. You don't know my situation. You have to help me. Please."

He went slack like an idiot at the sight of her tears. She immediately shoved her knee where sharp knees had no business going. Her elbow slammed into his chin, and before he could begin to breathe again, she was out from under him and running into the jungle, taking a split second to sweep down and pick up her own weapon.

What was wrong with him? He was the most cynical man he knew. He could usually smell a trap or a scam from a mile away. But something about her kept sneaking under his defenses.

He rolled to his feet and tore after her, limping, determined not to make the same mistake again. They were both playing with their lives like this, dammit. He couldn't see her in the darkness—the thick canopy above didn't let through much moonlight. He fired a warning shot in the general direction where he could hear her moving.

Then he could no longer hear her. Could he have shot her by accident? So much the better. Except, part of him didn't like the idea of Megan Cassidy dead, no matter how much grief she'd caused him. He caught himself. There he went again, thinking stupid thoughts.

He stole forward step by slow step. At last he spotted her figure emerging out of the darkness. She faced him head-on, her legs slightly apart, with her gun in both hands, aimed directly at him. A movie poster combination of dangerous and sexy. She made a fine-looking enemy, he had to give her that.

But he was done letting that affect him. He pointed his own gun right back at her. "Now what?"

"One of us shoots the other and gets what she wants." Everything about her was cocky, from her stance to her voice.

It turned him on, God help him. But he was a professional. "Juarez will kill Zak if he gets him back," he said, deciding to reason with her instead of using brute force and threats. He could always fall back on those. Maybe he could appeal to her feminine compassion. "He's just a kid."

For a moment she wavered. But only for a moment. "That's between the two of them."

All right, so she wasn't interested in compassion—not that big a surprise. Maybe she was interested in money. "I'll pay you for him."

"I'm not after money," she snapped, as if offended. "Why do you want the two-bit crook? You two business partners? He screwed the big boss over. He's going to do the same with you."

He thought for a long moment, trying to figure her out, then decided to take a calculated gamble. "He's not a two-bit crook, exactly. He's the son of a U.S. governor."

That gave her pause. "Which one?"

He told her, and again she wavered.

"The reward would be substantial." He pushed.

She didn't even bother to acknowledge that. "So you're U.S. law enforcement or something."

He calculated how far they'd come from Zak. Far enough. The kid should be out of hearing distance. "Or something."

For a second she took her eyes off him to scan the black jungle behind him. Her gun never moved, however. "Where is the rest of your team?"

"Where I come from, we don't waste a whole team's time on a quick little job like rescuing a politician's idiot son."

She considered him for a long time. "Are you one of Colonel Wilson's men?"

He went still. Now that was a question he hadn't expected. Who the hell was she? "How do you know Colonel Wilson?"

The Colonel headed the Special Designation Defense Unit, SDDU, a top secret team of commando soldiers who ran various secret missions around the globe without anyone knowing. So how did she know?

"You're not CIA. The FBI never sends just one man. If you were a mercenary, you wouldn't have helped me. There was no money in it," she added. "So that didn't leave much."

Sound logic. But it didn't explain how she'd come to know about his team. Very few people knew about the SDDU. A handful of top government officials, and the few FBI and CIA agents who'd done joint missions. Had she?

"Who do *you* work for?"

She pressed her generous lips into a tight line as she glared at him without saying anything.

"Have you infiltrated Juarez's band of criminals?" He couldn't help being a little impressed.

"You're ruining an undercover op a full year in the making," she snapped at him. "I need Zak."

He reported to the Colonel, not to anyone else. "You can't have him."

"There'll be a meeting between Juarez and the big boss, Don Pedro, next week. No outsider has ever been to the Don's secret stronghold before. We know he deals weapons to terrorists from there. I need to know what kind and how much. I need to uncover his connections. These are weapons that could march straight north, across Mexico and then through the U.S. border."

She was hunting terrorist connections abroad. A CIA spook then. He should have guessed. She'd ruled out the CIA for him first, because that was her outfit and if he was with them, she would have known it.

He was beginning to understand her better now. She was trusted at Juarez's camp, but not enough for Juarez to include her in his personal retinue. Except, if she did something his other men couldn't accomplish, like bringing back the kid who'd killed his brother-in-law...

Her plan wasn't bad. She was working on an important mission. But his orders weren't to accommodate other important missions he came across. He only had one order from the Colonel: to bring the governor's son back.

"I'm sorry," he said, and he meant it. "You'll find another way."

But instead of accepting defeat, she shot at his foot, apparently not done with this way yet. A miracle that she hadn't maimed him.

He had no choice but to shoot the gun out of her hand. He did just that, then lunged forward, and they went rolling on the ground again.

"This doesn't feel like progress." She had the presence of mind to joke with him, even though her hand must have smarted.

It might not have felt like progress, but it sure felt like one hundred percent pure, curvy female to Mitch. He wouldn't have minded the prolonged body contact so much if the ground wasn't full of danger. He couldn't afford to get injured, and he didn't want her hurt, either.

"Could we have a civilized discussion about this?" he suggested between a flip and a roll.

"Worried that you can't win by sheer force alone?" She grunted and heaved.

"Stop." He pinned her down at last. "You roll into a sharp branch and your mission goes nowhere."

She gave it another try before she stilled. "Fine. A civilized conversation it is. In the morning." She blew out a breath. "So you're an extractor."

"*The* extractor. When someone needs a target removed unseen from an impossible situation, I'm the go-to guy." She might as well know that he wasn't going to give up or give in to her.

"Do you always get them?"

"Always." He didn't compromise.

"It's that important to you. Interesting." She gave him a calculating look. "I'm guessing you lost someone close to you at one point?"

A discussion they weren't going to have. He moved back slowly and let her go, then offered her a hand.

She sprang up on her own and dusted off her clothes. "Just for the record, you called truce first."

She sauntered off toward her makeshift camp without looking back at him. Unfortunately, not enough moonlight filtered through the canopy for him to fully enjoy that tempting image.

"Take a picture. It'll last longer," she called over her shoulder.

She must have attended some CIA training on how to be thoroughly irritating. But if she thought she was going to be the last spy standing here, she was sadly mistaken.

He headed after her, hoping Zak hadn't done anything stupid like untying himself and running off into the jungle. They'd had enough excitement for one night.

As luck would have it, the kid was where they'd left him. Mitch checked his restraints and, despite loud demands, left them in place.

"Up," he ordered next, nudging Megan onto the platform and tying her wrist to the other end the same way she'd tied up Zak. Then he lay between them, snug, his gun resting on his chest, finger on the trigger.

He didn't like the idea of the other two guns, plus the machete, scattered out there, but he'd have to wait for daylight to look for them and secure them.

"You can't be serious about this." Megan snarled the words at him.

He settled into the uncomfortable bed. "Try to get some rest."

"There's not enough room," Zak grumbled. "Untie me now. You can't treat me like this. I'm the victim here."

"I could knock you out, if you prefer," he offered.

"You can't touch me. You're getting paid to save me."

"This is cozy. Think of us as one big happy family," he told the kid.

Megan turned to her side, jabbing him viciously in the side with her elbow in the process, probably not by accident.

He let it go. Couldn't be mad at her when they were pressed against each other full-length. She smelled like the rain forest and the cheap soap they'd all used at the guest-house. Not a combination that would turn the average man's head, but for some reason it got under his skin.

He shook off the tension that had pushed him forward since she'd left him tied to the sink. Then he grinned into the night as the breeze moved her hair and it tickled his chin. At least, chances were, he was going to have pretty good dreams.

An honest to goodness spook, looking like a teenage video gamer's dream come true. Thank God for small favors. When he'd thought she was a lost suburban housewife, he didn't know what to do with her. When he'd thought she was a heartless criminal, one of Juarez's lackeys, he didn't want anything to do with her. But now that it turned out that they were almost on the same side... Their chance encounter suddenly brimmed with possibilities.

For after.

When they were both done with their missions and back in the U.S., he wouldn't mind asking her out for a drink. He was ready to sink deeper into that fantasy when he heard something moving in the jungle, circling their small camp.

Megan heard it, too. She went instantly rigid.

So much for a good night's sleep.

"Give me your gun," she whispered under her breath.

Not going to happen. But he did reach up and untie her wrist. He had firsthand experience with the kind of damage she could inflict even unarmed. If they were attacked, she would be far from helpless. That was all he could do for her. He didn't trust her enough to arm her, at least not until he knew what kind of danger they faced.

He listened.

Four men. He used military hand signals to pass on the news.

She nodded and pointed west.

He slipped from the makeshift bamboo bed, pulled back into the jungle just as the four shadows snuck into the clearing opposite them. They moved forward, then one of them signaled to the others to stop.

Mitch was ready to open fire at the first

sign of aggression. He could take them out in a second.

"Is that you, *chica?* What are you doing here?" the one in the front asked with a voice raspy from too many cigarettes.

"Dammit, Paolo." She swore an impressive blue streak in Spanish. "Ever heard of giving warning? I almost shot you."

Megan jumped off the bed, brazen as anything, pretending to shove her nonexistent gun into the waistband at her back. And as dark as the night was, it seemed she managed to fool the others, because nobody called her on it.

If he weren't careful, he was going to start admiring her or something stupid like that, Mitch thought.

"I'm taking Juarez's young friend back to him," she told the men, tossing wood on the fire, looking around surreptitiously.

Paolo checked out the sleeping platform behind her. "We've been looking for the bastard all day. We made camp east of here a couple of hours ago. Upwind, or we would have smelled your fire. Heard the shots, though. Figured we better investigate." He knocked Zak to the ground and took his place.

The kid had to stay where he fell, with the ankle restraint still tethering him to the platform. He couldn't do much more than squat and look scared.

Paolo patted the bed next to him and flashed a grin at Megan. "How about you come back to bed?"

Mitch took a silent step forward. He wasn't quite out of cover, but he was close enough to take swift action if needed.

"How about you give up? As I said before, I don't mix business and pleasure."

"Give it a try, I promise you'll like it." Paolo's tone took on a menacing edge. There were four of them, and one of her. He probably knew that she, too, would have the odds figured. "Come on."

Mitch stepped into the clearing, not bothering with stealth. He wanted them to see him.

Immediately, four guns pointed at his chest. Four pairs of hard eyes said they wouldn't hesitate to pull the trigger.

"Friends of yours?" he asked Megan as if he'd just gotten back from a bathroom break.

"Who the hell is he?" Paolo came off the bed.

"An old friend." Megan stepped closer to

Mitch. "I knew he was in the area so I called him in for help."

"The boss don't like strangers in his business," Paolo warned her, then turned to Mitch. "Who do you work for?"

"Whoever pays best. Right now, I'm protecting a logging operation north of here." All logging in the area was illegal, so that should give him the right credentials. "Gun for hire, soldier of fortune, that kind of thing," he added.

"Which timber boss?" Paolo wanted to know.

Mitch kept his demeanor friendly and his hand close to the weapon tucked into his waistband. "He doesn't like his name passed around."

Tense silence stretched between them.

But when Paolo lowered his gun, so did the others. "Forget logging. You'll come with us. I know a man who pays well and needs some extra muscle."

And just like that, his chances of getting Zak out of the country swiftly and unnoticed dimmed. Sure, he'd taken on four men in a gunfight before. When he'd been on his own. But if all hell broke loose now, in the dark,

Zak or Megan could get killed, and he wasn't going to take that chance.

Under the smile on his face, his jaw clenched. Instead of taking Zak to safety, he was going to have to stand by as the men took the kid back to the lion's den.

Megan could have been helpful, but damned if he knew whether he could count on her. She seemed determined to care only about her own mission and nothing else. He had hoped to convince her once morning came, but they weren't likely to get time alone for that now.

And the balance of power had shifted anyway. The men had played right into her hand.

Regardless, he *would* get Zak home. *With or without her,* he thought as he surveyed the drug lord's lackeys for weaknesses. He never left a mission incomplete.

Chapter Four

By the time morning came, Mitch had a plan. He'd thought about it all night long as he'd slept in spurts squatting by the fire. He could take the men out during their long trek. Getting another look at Juarez's compound might have provided new intelligence he could pass on to the Colonel, but Megan had already seen the place and had probably passed on all kinds of intel to the CIA. They could deal with Juarez.

His job was to deal with the kid. Which meant he would have to take out Paolo and the others, then turn around and continue north with Zak. He'd call in for military transport the second he could make connection.

Megan Cassidy was welcome to do whatever she pleased. As long as she didn't stand in his way.

They marched forward silently, in single

file. Paolo led the way, with Sanchez, his second in command, behind him. Then came Megan, then Zak, then Mitch, then the other two men.

Mitch reached into the opening of his shirt and plucked a leech from under his collar, slowing his steps as he disposed of the little bloodsucker. He needed to fall to the back of the line. He didn't like anyone with a weapon behind him.

He made a point of scratching a couple of times before stopping altogether and stepping aside. "Damned leeches in my pants."

One of the men laughed at him, another winced with sympathy, the rest didn't bother to respond. Nobody stopped to wait. He messed around with his belt and zipper for a while, until they passed him, then he fell in step behind them.

Step one completed.

Yet the setup was far from ideal. Since they were walking single file, he'd have to take out the men in the back first as they blocked sight of the others up front. But if he took out the men in the back, the two in the front would start shooting at him. Which would leave Megan and Zak in the crossfire.

Not that she was a factor. Megan Cassidy

was nothing more to him than the possibility of some carnal fun. His unhelpful fascination with her had to stop before it got him in trouble. She could take care of herself. And yet, on some level, he cared. Not because she was another American; God knew he'd been stabbed in the back more than once by his own countrymen. And definitely not because she was CIA. He'd been caught up in their intrigues before. Their wheeling and dealing had once cost the life of a good friend and nearly his, too.

He had allegiance to his country, not to its corrupt systems. He took orders only from the Colonel. He was loyal only to his team. He trusted very few people beyond that circle. Friends outside the job were too much of a risk.

His family thought he was dead. Better that way for everyone. They hadn't gotten along too well when they'd thought he was alive. This way, his work didn't put them in danger, and they didn't get on each other's nerves.

He was too busy to be lonely.

Except, back when he'd thought Megan was a traumatized tourist he was leading out of the jungle, she'd sure made him wish for…

He wasn't sure what, but an empty little spot suddenly opened up in his chest.

He looked at her as she marched on resolutely and felt a funny kind of tingle on his skin.

Maybe he was getting jungle fever. That would explain why his thoughts were getting jumbled all of a sudden. He wasn't the type of man who lost his head, and consequently his life, over a pretty woman.

He had a small box of emergency medicine in his backpack, antibiotics and malaria pills among them. He'd take some meds when they next stopped, Mitch decided as he marched forward, watching where he stepped, until sharp cries pulled his attention to the canopy.

Howler monkeys were passing by high above the ground, flashes of gray streaking through the emerald green of the foliage. He watched them for a second before returning his focus to the path in front of him and the four men he had to neutralize before he could complete his mission.

"Are your wrists okay?" Megan was asking Zak up ahead. Paolo had tied the kid's hands thoroughly that morning. She checked his skin and reached into her backpack, pulled

out a jar and put some kind of a salve on
Zak's wrist.

The kid's response was lost in the noise the
monkeys made.

She was a strange one. Taking the kid
back to Juarez where he'd be shot, yet worried about the ropes cutting into his wrists.
She didn't seem hard-hearted. But definitely
focused. She would do whatever it took to
achieve her aim.

So would he.

The men looked up at the monkeys. Mitch
looked at the men. His best chance would be
if one of the two up front stopped for a bathroom break. Both at the same time would be
outstanding, but he wouldn't hold his breath
for that. He would take whatever opportunity
presented itself.

His break came sooner than he'd expected.
The howlers were crossing right above them.
The man in front of him slowed as a shot
went off.

Paolo had decided to go monkey hunting.
But he'd only managed to wound the animal,
which clung to a branch, emitting a keening
sound of pain.

Mitch took aim and ended the animal's
suffering. Then their line scattered at last,

Paolo going for the monkey, taking charge of it, even though it hadn't been his kill. "Let's eat!" Others moved off into the jungle to gather wood for a fire. Mitch used the distraction to get closer to Megan.

"Are you with me?" He kept his voice below a whisper. He felt better just standing next to her. Didn't understand why. He barely knew her. She'd scammed him.

A lock of hair had escaped her ponytail and curled against the scar on her neck. His fingers itched to tuck that lock behind her ear. He didn't.

He watched regret come into her eyes as she said, "I can't. Not in this."

So she wouldn't fight to help him. But would she fight against him? Or would she stay out of it all together? He didn't have a chance to ask.

"Hey, gringo," Paolo called him over, working at skinning the monkey. "Look at this. Big sucker, eh?" He puffed his chest out. "What do you think?"

"I think we're about to have some lunch." He faked an enthusiastic grin.

Twenty minutes later, the fire crackled under the roasting meat. When it was done, Paolo divided it and handed out the portions.

Mitch ate in silence, filling his stomach for the first time in two days. Now if he could only get some decent sleep. As soon as he and Zak could make their escape and get far enough away from Juarez, they were going to take a serious break.

From the corner of his eye, he caught Megan sneaking off into the woods. Probably for a bathroom break. The men had taken theirs as they'd walked, barely bothering to step off the path before aiming at the nearest tree.

Mitch gobbled up the rest of his portion, noting the position of every man, the whereabouts of every weapon. Now was his chance. He could take them without having to worry about Megan. He reached for his gun, ready to yell at Zak to duck.

If he weren't watching the men so closely, he wouldn't have caught the exchanged look between Paolo and Sanchez. A second later, Paolo melted into the jungle following the path Megan had disappeared down a minute ago.

"All right." Sanchez stood. "Better get going."

The others washed down their food with some water then picked up their backpacks and fell in line. One yanked Zak onto his feet. The kid shot a plaintive look at Mitch, but he was more concerned about why Paolo had taken off after Megan.

He made sure he was the last to head out, bringing up the rear. Then he silently fell behind without anyone noticing. They were slowed by the heat and humidity as much as their full bellies. Catching up with them again wouldn't be too difficult. Their job was to bring Zak back to Juarez, so unless the kid did something stupid, he'd be safe for the moment.

In five minutes, Mitch had returned to the remains of their abandoned fire, drops of water sizzling on the coals as rain began to fall. He moved forward in the direction Megan and Paolo had taken.

He was a pretty good tracker, and they hadn't bothered to mask their trail. Another minute or two brought him close enough to hear the two of them, and he soon realized they weren't talking. They were fighting. Mitch rushed forward, finding them rolling in the undergrowth, glaring and swearing at each other. Paolo was doing his best to gain the upper hand while Megan fought like crazy to prevent that from happening. They were a blur of growling faces and entangled limbs.

For a moment he hesitated, unsure if Megan would want him to interfere or if she needed to beat the man herself to maintain her status on the team. He didn't want to mess up her mission if he didn't have to.

But then Paolo grabbed her between the legs and reason flew from Mitch, a swift wave of anger pushing him forward without allowing him time to think. The cold fury that leaped to life inside his belly surprised him. "Get your hands off her."

Paolo glanced back with a dark look on his weather-beaten face. "You wait your turn."

Two more steps forward and Mitch was lifting him off her, tossing him aside with more force than was necessary. He went for his gun at the same time as Paolo. Mitch squeezed the trigger first.

The shot rent the silence and sent birds flying. Monkeys screeched in the distance. Paolo's eyes went wide and stayed that way.

"And now how are we going to explain this?" Megan's cheeks turned pink with outrage. She didn't seem to notice or care about her injuries, but the welts on her neck and forehead pumped a fresh supply of anger through Mitch.

His jaw tightened. "How badly are you hurt?"

She was on her feet already and searching for her gun among the decaying leaves. She found it, stashed it, then stamped over to Paolo.

Mitch didn't need to check the body. He always hit what he aimed at. If he meant for a man to be dead, the bastard was dead. End of story.

Paolo no longer held his attention. Megan did.

"Shot through the heart. Great." Annoyance roughened her voice. "You had to do that? Seriously?"

Her clothes were wet and muddy, outlining her tempting figure. She shook some stray leaves from her hair with an impatient flick of her head. "Did I ask for help? I could have handled it."

He hadn't expected gratitude, but he didn't deserve getting chewed out for what he'd done, either. "Forget I came back."

He tried to stare her down, but she stared right back, holding his gaze without flinching. She was fierce and wild, and he had the sudden impulse to stride right up to her, yank her into his arms and kiss her. Anger and frustration morphed into hot lust in the blink of an eye. He wanted to feel those full lips crushed under his, wanted a taste of her.

Whoa. Rein it in. He stood down and shook his harebrained impulses right out of his head. For one thing, she'd just been attacked. She sure didn't need more of the same from anyone. For another, even if she were willing, even if she were begging for his touch, he needed to stay *far* away from her. He was here on a top secret mission, not on some singles vacation.

Her chin sunk back down, her shoulders too, as she calmed herself. "How is your shoulder? I didn't want to ask in front of the others this morning."

She didn't want to alert them to any potential weakness on his part. Smart. Too bad he was beyond appreciating the gesture just now.

"Forget it." Lust and frustration had him on edge. He turned on his heels and marched away.

She caught up quickly. She, too, seemed to be humming with tension. "We'll tell Sanchez that we heard people moving through the woods and Paolo went to investigate, sending us back to let the others know. He'll expect Paolo to catch up eventually. When he doesn't, he'll assume that some wild animal or one of Cristobal's men got him."

He didn't like it that she came up with a plan first. Ever since they'd met, she'd always been a step ahead of him. It bothered him more than it should have. Why? He occasionally worked on teams. He wasn't always the best and the quickest. But with her—

Was he trying to impress her? Now that would be stupid.

"How about the gunshot?" he thought suddenly. "They had to have heard that."

"Maybe not. The vegetation is thick enough to swallow the sound. There's a river up ahead. If they were close enough to it when your gun went off, the sounds of the water could have drowned out the shot."

They followed the trail in silence for a while, until it stopped on the bank of a river she'd been talking about. For a second he wondered if it was the same one they'd crossed yesterday, winding its way through the jungle. If it was, then they were farther upstream. The riverbed was narrower and shallower than where they'd crossed before. Then he noticed a deep gouge in the sand that showed where a canoe had recently been pulled into the water.

Oh, hell, no.

They could only see a few hundred feet ahead where the river disappeared around a bend. No trace of the men anywhere.

He swore. This couldn't be happening. He slammed his backpack into the mud as steam gathered inside him.

"Juarez has boats and weapons stashed all over the jungle in case of emergency." Megan's voice was filled with a level of frustration that matched his. "I left an ATV twenty miles or so from here. I was hoping Paolo would lead us that way, but of course he had to choose otherwise. Now we have no choice but to follow the river."

He stared at the water, his mood getting darker by the second. The men were gone and they'd taken Zak along with them. He paced the shore, not quite able to believe it. He'd saved Megan, who didn't in the least want to be saved, and in the process he'd lost the kid.

HE LOOKED LIKE he was ready to strangle her. Fine, so she'd stolen Zak from him at that guesthouse. But, hey, nobody told him to rush to rescue her from Paolo. "You should have stayed with the kid and made them wait."

His lips narrowed further. His nostrils flared. He reminded her of a bull in the arena, pawing the ground. All in all, she preferred this look to the one he'd presented back in the woods.

Back there, he'd looked like the hero out of some big-budget Hollywood action flick as he'd broken through the bushes and challenged Paolo. She wasn't used to rescue. She couldn't say her heart hadn't fluttered just a little. It must have been some basic, primitive female reaction to the macho display of an alpha male. But she didn't appreciate the interference, and she definitely didn't appreciate the flutter. That simply couldn't happen again.

Mitch Mendoza was nothing but a giant monkey wrench in her plans. That he was hot was beside the point. She'd just have to ignore the way her hormones stood up to salute him every time she looked at him.

Because of him, Paolo was dead, and his absence might make Juarez suspicious, regardless of her cover story. And now she wouldn't be the one to bring Zak to the mighty drug lord. Sanchez would get the credit instead.

No way. She *had* to get the brownie points.

Juarez had to take her with him to see Don Pedro.

Her mind flipped through all the possibilities until she hit upon an idea that might work. "There are some rapids up ahead. They'll have to take the canoe out of the water and carry it around. It'll make them lose whatever time they gained on the river. If we move fast enough, we can catch up to them."

He rolled his neck and his shoulders, adjusted his backpack. "Let's move out," he called, taking the lead.

Typical man.

When she tried to cut in front of him— hello, she was the one who knew the terrain, she'd traipsed all over this jungle in the past year—he picked up speed to prevent her.

Fine. She fell in line behind him. Carrying that massive ego around was going to get too heavy sooner or later. He followed the river, logically, so he wasn't leading them off course. She could afford to humor him. One of them had to be the mature adult. With eight younger brothers, she was used to the role. She could handle it.

"So, out of curiosity," he asked over his shoulder, "you would have let Paolo beat you up or worse to keep your cover?"

"This happens to be an important mission." But that was only part of it. She worked for the CIA, but she had her own reasons for being here. Reasons that would likely end her government career when the truth came out. The home office didn't appreciate operatives with private agendas, regardless of the worthiness of their cause.

"You're tough."

His acknowledgment meant nothing. She squashed the small thrill she got from it. "Don't you forget it."

"Tough for a girl, I mean."

"Well, that just ends all the goodwill we've been building," she deadpanned.

"A sense of humor, too." He mocked her. "So with all that, how come you're not in a safer job in a nicer place?"

"I'm exactly where I want to be."

"All things considered, I'd rather be on my couch with a cold beer, watching a game on the big screen."

She didn't believe him for a second. He had the look of a man who lived for action. He was always on, always ready, mind and body honed in combat. You didn't get this good at something without liking it. "How often does that happen?"

"Once a year if I'm lucky."

She didn't know much about him, only that he was one of Colonel Wilson's men. The Colonel was running some commando group that flew so deep under the radar, even Congress didn't know about it. Which was a neat way to avoid congressional oversight, she supposed. They did lone-wolf operations, deep undercover, took care of problems nobody else dared to tackle.

The grand sum of her knowledge about the team didn't amount to much, despite the fact that at one point, she'd tried all her CIA resources to find out more. She'd been stunned at how fast doors had been slammed in her face.

Clearly they were in the black op business. She wasn't impressed. The U.S. had enough law enforcement and military branches already. They didn't need a new batch of yahoos who thought they were above the law and interfered in the legitimate agencies' business. And it was dangerous, too. She thought of Jamie at home, of the way he was now. Sorrow filled her swiftly. She put thoughts of her eldest brother away.

"Why don't you go home?" she suggested to Mitch. "After I'm done with what I've come to accomplish, I'll take Zak back to the U.S. with me."

"You'd leave him behind in the blink of an eye."

She shrugged. "He's grown on me."

He shot back on amused look. "How about me?"

"You leave now, and I'll let you know if I miss you in a couple of weeks."

He snorted. Then he got serious. "Without me, Zak will be dead within ten minutes of reaching that compound."

"I'll keep an eye on him."

"He's not your top priority."

He was right about that. She was here to rescue someone else. So she changed the subject. "How long have you been in the commando business?"

"Too long. How long you've been with the company?"

"Since college."

"Spook University?"

"Yale."

He gave her the once-over. "Come from big money?"

"No money at all and nine kids in the family. Went to school on scholarship."

"You must be the eldest."

"How did you know?"

"Bossy and stubborn."

She looked at the ground for something to throw at his wide back and found nothing but composting leaves. "I grew up with eight younger brothers. They needed positive direction. Anyway, being decisive is a positive trait."

"All the bossiness could be the reason why you don't have a man. Ever thought of that?" He was baiting her on purpose now. He seemed to get some sick satisfaction out of needling her.

"I've got someone back home."

"You haven't been home in over a year," he reminded her.

Not that she needed a reminder. Her relationship with Vincent hadn't been that great to start with. She had no illusions about him waiting for her. Not when she hadn't been able to tell him where she was going or how long she would be staying.

"I'm sure your life is chock-full of women," she shot back.

"You have no idea how grateful some of those damsels in distress I save can be." He smirked. "You realize that since we've met, I've saved you once a day?"

Okay, he'd gone too far with that one. She didn't need saving. Ever. Her self-sufficiency was a matter of pride. He was possibly the most infuriating man she'd ever seen, and she had eight brothers to compare him to, not to mention dozens of colleagues. She did work in a male-dominated field.

"The first time around, you weren't saving me, I was scamming you." She set the record straight. "And if you'd stayed with Zak instead of interfering with Paolo, we wouldn't have lost the kid." She would have been able to fight Paolo off. Probably.

If she hadn't rolled her eyes, she wouldn't have noticed the movement on the branch above Mitch. He didn't. He'd been paying too much attention to annoying her and missed the snake. Just as it dropped out of the tree, she leaped forward and swiped at it with her machete.

He spun, alerted by the noise she made. The snake's body fell around his neck with a small thud, the head landing at his feet. He stood frozen to the spot, wide-eyed, color creeping into his stubble-covered cheeks.

"You scared of snakes?" Megan smiled. So he did have a chink in his armor. She softened a little, closing the remaining distance between them with a short step and slipping the still-wriggling body from around his neck to throw it into the underbrush. "No good for eating. This kind has a bitter taste."

His chestnut eyes were way too close.

His gaze fell to her lips.

The jungle heated around them. Breathing seemed extra difficult for a moment.

An electric charge ran through her. She wasn't sure what she should hope for, that he'd kiss her or that he wouldn't.

His tongue darted out and moistened his lower lip. His Adam's apple bobbed up, then back down as he swallowed.

Then he stepped away.

SHE HAD NO IDEA how hot she was. How was that possible? She about short-circuited his brain every time he looked at her. Seeing her in action… She had to be getting male attention 24/7 at Juarez's camp. Of course, it was probably unwanted attention, more worrisome than self-esteem boosting. Or downright dangerous, like Paolo had been.

"Thank you," he told her as he moved forward. "That's what you do when someone saves your life, by the way. Acknowledge it instead of denying it."

"If you ever save my life, I'll be sure to express my gratitude," she said in snarky tone behind him.

He allowed himself a small grin. He didn't normally work with a partner. She was annoying at times, definitely tested his patience on occasion, but she was also entertaining. And hot. Something about her made hormones flood his brain. *Great.* He was in the middle of a mission. He'd lost his charge. And now his thoughts made him feel like a teenager.

He'd better fix that and quickly, before he kissed her or did something equally stupid. The snake hadn't bothered him, but when she'd stepped that close—to be that near to those lips…

They marched on in silence for a while, pushing as hard as they could. He walked in front. Walking behind her would have provided too much distraction. He needed to keep his mind clear and keep up the pace. Catching up with the men before they reached the compound was crucial.

They didn't even stop when they came up on a mango tree. They filled their pockets as they walked. Their forced march expended a lot of energy. Replacing that was vital to remain in top fighting shape. They ate as they hiked, but also saved some for later.

She never complained once. Not about the unforgiving pace he set, not about the lack of food or lack of breaks. About an hour later, they heard the rapids, but couldn't see much. The area around them was too overgrown with bamboo to walk, so they had to turn deeper into the jungle. Long minutes ticked by before they could begin angling back toward the river.

They reached the water just as Sanchez and the others were getting ready to give the final push to their canoe on the other side. Zak was already sitting in the front, looking haggard.

"Hey," Sanchez called over the water, straightening when he spotted them, his right hand lingering by his gun. "Where is Paolo?"

Had they heard the shot, was the question.

Mitch stayed quiet, letting Megan take the lead and make explanations. They trusted her more than him. She had quite a way with words when she was trying to annoy him. Let her use all that verbal creativity on Sanchez and talk her way out of trouble.

But instead of telling her little tale, she opened fire without warning.

She never did what he expected her to do. Absolutely never. The woman was bewildering.

Sanchez went down first, then the man behind him. Mitch, recovered at last, took care of the third.

"They would have never believed us. Zak wasn't in the way. I knew I could do it without him getting hurt—" Megan began to explain, but fell silent when the kid began screaming, drawing their attention.

"Help!" He scrambled to keep his balance as the water got hold of the canoe and pulled it from shore. The boat wobbled, got stuck for a moment, then jerked farther away as the current took hold.

He stared back at them with horror on his face as the swift waters carried him downriver.

Without a paddle.

This must be some gigantic, cosmic joke, Mitch thought as he stared after his charge.

Except it wasn't at all funny.

Chapter Five

"Jump," Megan shouted to Zak, as she took off running. She kept one eye on him and one on where she stepped. "Jump and swim."

But the kid looked too scared to do anything.

Mitch passed her. He wasn't as much running as leaping from safe spot to safe spot. The riverbank was littered with rocks and logs and all sorts of rubble the water had deposited. Nature's hazard course.

She pushed as hard as she could, but not as hard as he did. One of them had to be safe. If he got injured, she was the backup.

He ripped off his backpack and tossed it so he could go faster. When she reached it, she picked it up. She would catch up with them eventually.

She kept him in sight for another five minutes before the rocky bank gave way to flatter, muddy terrain and he disappeared into denser foliage. She could hear him for a little longer as he dashed through the brush. After that, she heard nothing.

A bend in the river took the kid from her sight, too. Then she was alone in a massive green labyrinth of danger. She kept her gun handy, mindful of wild animals as she ran on, alert and determined. Albeit not one hundred percent sure what in the hell she was doing.

The kid was gone down the river, and she'd let Mitch go after him. Had trusted him. Treated him like a teammate. The thought occurred to her suddenly. She wasn't a fan of teammates, frankly.

She didn't mind helping others. She just didn't like them helping her, didn't like relying on them. She preferred to do things for herself. Maybe because she was a woman in a male-dominated field and didn't want to appear weak.

It wouldn't be good if she began relying on Mitch now.

She pushed harder. The man had a way of getting under her skin. He better not think that if he got to Zak first, he'd have some kind of a claim on him. She was taking the kid back to Juarez. End of story.

If Mitch didn't like that, tough for him.

She should have shot him at the guest-house. Not killed him or anything, but hurt him enough to make sure he wouldn't be coming after her. Or, at the very least, she should have tied him to a tree after he'd shot Paolo. Coming back to Sanchez alone, she could have claimed that the two men took each other out. Sanchez would have accepted that. He would have come across the river for her, and she could have gone back to Juarez with the men.

Mitch was a major complication for her mission, but every time she had a chance to get rid of him, she hadn't. Better not be because he was ridiculously attractive. That would be crazy. She would never let a consideration that shallow affect her mission. It didn't matter that he was hot. Or that he was good at what he did. Though she respected that. But the appreciation she had for him was strictly professional. Okay, mostly professional.

All right, so fine, she wasn't a saint.

She did like him. But she also wanted to strangle him. Frequently.

He'd come to help her with Paolo. Which had been a mistake. But the salient fact was that he'd been with Zak, the object of his rescue mission, and he'd left the kid to come after her because he'd thought she was in trouble.

A sweet gesture, as much as she hated to admit it. Not that she wanted sweet.

She didn't need a protector. She managed just fine on her own. She didn't want a partner.

Yet here he was, a thorn in her side.

She was carrying his backpack for heaven's sake, like some moonstruck teenage boy carried books to a high school girl's locker. And her thoughts kept buzzing around him.

A noise ahead drew her attention. She slowed and pulled her weapon. Heard swearing, followed by "It's me."

"Mitch?" She inched forward, ready for anything.

"I'm alone. It's okay."

She pushed through some sticky-leaved palms she hoped weren't poisonous and saw him at last.

He was sitting on a fallen tree, pressing leaves against a gash in his leg. "Broken stick of bamboo got me."

She dropped their bags at his feet and assessed the situation. Decent cut, but not life-threatening. "Zak?"

"Lost him."

That couldn't happen. Simply couldn't. Everything depended on her gaining Juarez's goodwill, and Zak was the only ace up her sleeve. "Did he ever jump out of the canoe?"

"Not that I saw."

She went for her emergency pack. For a split second she considered just tossing it to him and moving on.

Oh, fine. This didn't have to take long. She pulled out some gauze and antibiotic ointment and went to work, trying to ignore the way her fingertips tingled every time they touched his skin, which was tanned and smooth with plenty of hard muscles underneath. He was so quintessentially male, everything that was female in her responded to him.

For a second she imagined his hands on her, and the image took her breath away. But that could never happen. He was a big enough distraction already.

Pulling her mind in another direction took effort, but she did it. "In ten miles or so, there are more rapids." She tried to picture the spot. She'd only been there once. A dangerous place from what she could remember.

Mitch eyed the gun at her feet. "When did your backpack get filled up anyway? I checked it when you first showed up. You didn't have any weapons."

"Remember when I went back to the bushes to give back my breakfast?"

He winced. Then his eyes narrowed. "You hid everything important before you stepped out into the clearing. Then, after I checked, you went back and repacked. You weren't even sick?"

She smiled at him. Patted the bandage. "Done. That's the second time I saved your life, by the way." She stood, needing a little space after all that nearness.

"The snake wasn't that poisonous."

Still, he would have been *very* uncomfortable. She doubted that he could have walked out of the jungle unaided. "Fine. Once then." She could be reasonable.

"I have antibiotics in my backpack, too."

"You only have your backpack because I brought it after you." Would it have killed him to acknowledge that she'd been helpful?

He tested his leg then put his full weight on it. "All right. You saved my life. Want a reward?"

She hated that her body tingled at the prospect, even though the question had been meant as a put-down, not as a come-on.

"Sure." She swung her backpack on her back. "There's one thing I'd really like."

He gave her a careful look. Then a surprised glint came into his eyes that said he was starting to understand her unspoken thoughts. His lips stretched into a slow grin.

There was nothing for them there but trouble. Her heart rate picked up. Thank God, he couldn't see that.

"As a reward, you could stay out of my way." She turned on her heels and left him.

SHE WAS SASSY. He hadn't thought he'd liked that in a woman, but he couldn't remember the last time he enjoyed anyone's company this much. He was beginning to rethink the whole lone-wolf thing.

Maybe I could work with her, Mitch thought, as he tried not to think of the dozens of other things he would like to do with Megan Cassidy, none of them appropriate for two government operatives on duty.

Especially not with Zak missing.

He grabbed his own bag and took off after her. "So how bad are those rapids?"

"He'll be out of the canoe. Can he swim?"

He'd never thought to ask. "No idea." If the kid couldn't swim…

"I can't believe you lost him." She stomped forward.

"I lost him?" Just like a woman to blame a man for everything.

"I left him with you."

"You know, everything was going just fine until we met up with you." He'd found the compound without trouble, gotten the kid out, he'd even caught up with those troublesome witnesses. It hadn't been the smoothest op he'd ever handled, but he was managing.

Then came Megan Cassidy.

She said something under her breath that he couldn't hear and was pretty sure he didn't want to.

"You do realize that you're the biggest obstacle to my mission?" he asked her. "Not the jungle, not the bad guys. Trouble follows you. I've heard of people like that. They don't make it long in this business."

"Trouble doesn't follow me. I follow trouble. I go where trouble is, because that's my job. I conquer trouble."

"Is that how you got that scar?" He'd been curious about that from the first time he'd seen it.

"At the beginning, when I showed up at

Juarez's camp, the other men didn't exactly like the idea of me joining their team."

But she hadn't let that stop her. He was beginning to think that she was the type who didn't let anything stop her when she wanted something. Not a comforting thought since, in this case, they both wanted the same thing. And only one of them could have the kid.

He was definitely taking Zak. As far as all the other things he wanted where she was concerned went, he was going to forget about those. She was too much trouble. Why did he have to meet her?

Or, a better question was, why did he have to want her?

The admission didn't please him, but there it was. He wanted Megan Cassidy, undercover CIA spook, bane of his existence, destroyer of his mission. When she'd said she wanted a reward from him…his mind had jumped to all the wrong conclusions. The images that had flooded his brain… He couldn't go there. Their uneasy alliance was complicated already.

There was only one way to handle the situation. He was going to completely ignore the attraction and deny his misguided needs.

"Want a mango?" she called back.

Fruit, in fact, was not on the top of his list of desires. "Still got one." He patted his pocket, mindful of the whole apple-and-Eve motif.

His new wound pulled with every step he took. Normally, he would have ignored that, but now he focused on the pain to keep his thoughts from Megan. A light rain began to fall, and the bugs around them quieted, looking for shelters under leaves. Birds pulled their necks in. For a while, the only sound they could hear was the patter of raindrops on all that green. He didn't like the idea of getting soaked to the skin again. He'd barely been dry since he'd gotten here.

She marched on without complaint. He did the same.

He didn't ask her what she would do if they didn't find Zak. And she didn't ask him. For people like them, failure wasn't an option. Which meant more trouble down the line, sure confrontation.

She stopped suddenly.

He went for his weapon and scanned their surroundings.

"What is it?" He kept his voice at a whisper.

"Banana spider." She pointed.

"Poisonous." He'd seen them before, avoided them like the plague. Their poison was rarely strong enough to bring down a healthy adult, but it could cause considerable damage. And excruciating pain. The most painful spider bite on the planet, according to the experts. "Go around it slowly."

She did. "There must be banana trees around here somewhere." Her tone was wistful. She scanned the jungle once she was past the spider. A little potassium would have been nice. Fighting their way through the jungle took a lot out of them.

The six-inch hairy arachnid stood its ground and stared at them. Mitch followed Megan, keeping an eye on the ground around them on the principle that where there was one spider, there might be more. "Nasty thing."

She glanced back with an amused look. "I thought as a man you'd show more appreciation for it."

He raised an eyebrow.

"Priapism is one of the side effects of its bite."

He took a double take at the spider. Priapism, huh? How come that hadn't been in his training field book?

Priapism. He shook his head. Some guys might think something like that would be fun, but it sounded painful to him. He was happy with the way his body ordinarily worked.

He didn't need any stimulators, not with Megan walking in front of him, her pants wet from the rain and sticking to her body. She had to know it, but didn't seem self-conscious. She was focused on the job at hand.

He was focused on her shapely behind. He should have never let her walk in front of him.

Since they were near the river now, more light reached the ground and the undergrowth grew thicker. The green obstacle course didn't faze her any. She sure knew how to use that machete.

They tried to keep the river in sight, but saw no sign of Zak for the next few miles. They ate the last mangoes from their pockets, save one. He offered to take the lead. She handed him the machete and let him. She was self-sufficient and stubborn, but smart enough to know what was best for progress.

They walked another mile before they heard the cry. "Help! Help me!"

Zak. They pushed forward. At least ten minutes passed before they found him on the shore, stuck between two large rocks, half in, half out of the water, floundering like a giant, battered fish.

They rushed to him together, careful of the slippery rocks.

"I thought I was going to die." Zak shouted in between two moans. "What took you so long? My father is paying you to take better care of me than this."

Mitch held his rising ire, not the least because the kid was at least partially right. He extracted Zak and supported his weight as they walked to a more even spot where he could sit. He watched for a while as Megan carefully checked the kid over, then he took their water bottles and filled them up, grateful for the filter top that stood between them and the thousands of bacteria and microscopic parasites that lived in these waters.

"So you jumped?" Megan felt the kid's skull. "Minor gashes," she informed them when she was done.

"The water overturned the canoe. I could have drowned. You should have been with me," he accused Mitch. "When my father hears—"

"Shut up and be grateful you're alive," Megan snapped at him.

The kid pulled his neck in and blinked at her. "I'm hungry. Do we have any meat?"

She pulled a half a mango from her pocket.

"I don't think that's sanitary."

She shook her head and rolled her eyes at Mitch. "Maybe we'll run into some lemon ants."

"Are they yellow?" The kid wanted to know.

"They taste like lemons. You collect enough, it's a nice little shot of protein," she explained.

"Come on." Mitch stood. "Anyone coming down the river can see us here."

"I can't go anywhere." The kid dug his heels in. "I'm bruised and exhausted."

Mitch looked at him for a long second. To think that they were fighting over this little pile of— Seriously? He bent and tossed the kid over his shoulder then walked into the jungle with him.

Megan was saying something in the back, but the river drowned out her words. He could swear he heard *tubes* and *tied* both mentioned in the sentence.

Once they were back under thick cover, he set the kid down. He wasn't going to carry Zak's lazy behind, not unless the kid was truly incapacitated.

"We'll take a break." He rolled a log to

check under it for anything dangerous before they sat down.

"Spider!" Zak scrambled away, showing a lot more energy suddenly.

Mitch used a leaf the scoop the little thing up and shoo it out of harm's way. When he sat, the others followed his example. "You should have seen the banana spider we ran into on the way here."

"Tastes like bananas?" Zak asked, his face scrunched in a grimace.

"Not like lemon ants. The spiders live in banana trees. You wouldn't want one of those to bite you."

"Deadly?"

"Could be. Hurt like hell for sure. And according to Miss Know-it-all here, they cause priapism."

"Pria-what?"

"An erection that lasts hours," Megan put in, an amused look on her face. She was no doubt entertained by the fact that particular information had got stuck in Mitch's head.

The kid perked right up. "Can we go back to look at it?"

Megan struggled to hide a grin.

They took the rest of their five-minute break in silence. Zak looked thoughtful. He was probably calculating how much money he could make if he took a couple of banana spiders back to his frat brothers.

"Time to go." Mitch stood at last, realizing suddenly that they were at a decision point. He needed to take the kid north; Megan wanted to take him south. They were going to have to come to an agreement before they could proceed any farther.

"I need sleep. I haven't slept in ages," Zak pleaded.

He did look used up and wrung out. Either they could take an hour to rest here, or he'd slow them down so much they'd lose that hour, or more, anyway.

Mitch looked at Megan. She nodded.

He tossed his backpack to the kid. "Put this under your head."

"I thought we were supposed to sleep off the ground. What if something bites me?"

"Make a nest from a couple of large leaves. You'll be fine for a quick nap. I'll make sure nothing gets near you."

The kid looked doubtful, but settled down. He was asleep in two minutes.

Megan stood and took a few steps back. She checked her gun. But when she was done, she didn't put it away. "You should leave now."

A second passed before he caught on to what she was saying. Looked like the negotiation was about to begin. His hand crept toward his own weapon. "I'm taking the kid north."

"We're going south. We'll be at Juarez's camp by nightfall."

He stood slowly. "There'll be other opportunities to gain the man's trust."

"Not before the big meeting."

"There'll be other big meetings. Zak only has one life." He moved closer little by little as he talked.

She stood her ground, but lifted her weapon. "Leave. Get your backpack. Walk away."

"You would shoot the man who saved your life? Twice?" He tried to add some humor into the situation.

Her upper lip twitched. She said nothing.

"Seriously? You'd kill me." He stole another step closer and saw hesitation in her eyes.

A second later, her tough-chick face was back. "I wouldn't have to kill you. I'd just make sure you aren't in any shape to argue with me."

"You'd leave me wounded in the jungle?" He gained another foot.

"Something tells me you've survived worse."

Then he was close enough and he lunged. He'd meant to take her to the ground and wrestle the gun away from her, but she twisted at the last second and her back ended up slamming against the nearest tree. He was holding her gun hand up, pressing his body hard against hers to hold her still.

They were nose to nose, gazes clashing.

Her breath came in quick, hot spurts, her breasts pressing against his chest. He was so focused on that sensation that a second passed before he became aware of the sharp object in his back.

Her free hand was holding a small knife. Where had she been hiding that? He'd thought he'd already seen all her weapons.

"Let me go." She squirmed.

His body responded predictably.

Her eyes went wide. Then she gave a pained smile. "Look who doesn't need a banana spider."

Damn straight.

He kissed her, more to annoy her than to seduce her. The time and place wasn't exactly right for that, although, if they met again under different circumstances, he was going to revisit that option.

The knife pressed harder between his ribs. Her knee came up...stopped. Then went down. The pressure of the knife lessened, then disappeared.

Next thing he knew, she was kissing him back. Her lips went from resisting to softening to demanding in a heartbeat. He let go of her gun hand so he could palm her breasts. They fit his hands perfectly.

Hard heat suffused his body. And need.

His head was spinning with it.

Something cold pressing against his forehead brought him back to his senses. And after a dazed moment he realized that she was now holding the gun to his temple while the tip of her knife was at his side now, just a few inches from his heart.

"Reach behind you, slowly, pull out your gun and toss it into the woods," she ordered him.

She was so good. He found it difficult to be mad at her for that. There was such a thing as admiring a worthy enemy.

He pulled back enough to look into her eyes. Instead of the triumph he'd expected, he found only desperation in her gaze. Odd. He would have, at the very least, expected her to rub his defeat in his face. She did seem to enjoy watching him suffer.

"What's wrong?" He tried not to look at her swollen lips.

"You," she said without hesitation. "You shouldn't be here. There's no way for this to end well. If I want Zak, I'm going to have to hurt you."

"I'm not letting Zak go. He's my mission. I don't leave a mission incomplete. If you want to take him you're going to have to do more than hurt me. You're going to have to kill me." He took a big step back and went for his gun.

They faced off, both knowing there was no chance either of them would miss from this distance. It bothered him more than it should have, that's for sure.

"Come with me," he offered suddenly, surprised to hear the words come out. But once they were, he went with them. "To hell with the CIA. This is a suicide mission. Juarez will figure out who you are sooner or later. If this is the kind of work you want to do, we'll talk to Colonel Wilson."

She looked away for a second, blinked hard. "I need to do this. For my own reasons. This goes beyond the CIA."

That had his mind scrambling. "You're a double agent?" He shouldn't have been surprised. She was nothing if not full of surprises. But hell, he hadn't seen this coming. "You work for Cristobal?"

"I have a private mission. In addition to the official one. Nothing to do with any of the crime lords in the district."

So she hadn't gone completely rogue. Good. He wasn't sure how that would have influenced his decision. "Love, revenge or money?" he tried to narrow it down.

"I'm here for someone."

Love then. The thought caused an uncomfortable feeling in his chest. He hated the idea of her risking her life for a man. He hated the idea of her caring about another man that much.

Stupid.

She wasn't his.

But he wanted her to be, he realized now. Wanted her for more than a quick adventure. *But it isn't going to happen.* The resolution didn't make him hate the idea of another man any less, unfortunately. "Is he worth dying for?"

"I have no intention of dying. Come with me." She turned his offer on him. "All I need is three days. I need to go to Don Pedro's lair and get my brother. Then we grab Zak and we're out of there."

Brother. A knot relaxed deep inside him.

"What's he doing with the Don?" Hopefully his motives for being here were less misguided than Zak's.

"He works for the DEA. He was injured on his first international mission and disappeared. For the longest time we thought he was dead. Then there was a snippet of intel that Don Pedro was holding someone who fits his description." Her face transformed as she talked, her features softening as she spoke about her brother, then hardened again. "I'm not going home without Billy."

"And the CIA has no idea why you're really here." They wouldn't be amused when they found out. They liked to have their agents' full attention and loyalty. Undivided.

She shook her head.

He thought it over. "The man they're talking about, he might not be your brother."

Hurt flashed across her face. "I know he is. I can't explain how I know, but I do." She sounded defiant and at the same time desperate for him to believe her.

"Juarez might not take you."

"I'll find a way."

"You're asking me to risk this life—" he pointed at Zak "—for some cowboy mission that has a chance in a thousand of succeeding."

Her amber eyes held his. "Three days."

Part of him would have given her anything when she looked at him like that. But the trained soldier inside him knew better. "I can't."

"Do you have a brother?"

"My family has nothing to do with this." He didn't talk about his family. He didn't even think of them if he could help it. Except Cindy—who was lost to him.

"You come with me. I'll vouch for you with Juarez. You'll stay at the compound and make sure nothing happens to Zak. As soon as we're off to the meeting, you grab him and take him home. I'm not asking you to abandon your mission. I'm only asking for a brief delay."

He tried to think. He knew what he had

to do. Trouble was, it wasn't what he wanted to do. He wanted to help her. But before he could come to a decision, noises reached them from the jungle.

He lifted a hand, silencing her. A group of men were stomping through the woods, talking and swearing. Not entirely unexpected since they were a half day's walk from Juarez's camp. There would be some traffic.

They came closer and closer, until nothing separated them from Mitch but a dense stand of bamboo. He stood motionless, barely breathing as he listened to their bragging and banter. They were on their way back, having collected debts from the villages upriver. From the way they were talking, Mitch felt sorry for the villagers.

With a little luck, they would pass right by. The vegetation was thick, visibility terrible. Both Megan and he were dressed in clothes that blended into the jungle. They both stood stock-still.

The men reached them, then passed by.

"Who the hell are they?" Zak asked from his makeshift bed, awakening at the worst possible moment.

All movement halted immediately. The men stopped talking.

A branch snapped. Then another. They were spreading out.

Mitch pulled back, gun in hand, his blood boiling with frustration. He and Megan took a protective stance, the two of them making sure they had Zak covered. Like a team. Keeping Zak safe was still his number one objective. He had to remind himself of that. Because, at the moment, all he wanted was to shoot the twit.

Chapter Six

They were surrounded in minutes. Then ominous silence settled over the area once again. Megan's fingers twitched on the trigger.

Suddenly, she spotted movement to her right.

She swung that way.

"Que pasa, chica?" A tall, Creole man stepped from cover first. Umberto. He was one of the oldest men on Juarez's team. "Everything okay here?"

Megan made herself lower her weapon and put a smile on her face that she hoped looked real. "We're on our way back."

Since Umberto hadn't been in camp when Zak broke out, she relayed how the kid had some trouble with Juarez and ran away into the jungle, then how she'd hooked up with Mitch, her mercenary friend, for some help.

As she spoke, nine other men came forward, their rifles slung on their shoulders.

They took their cue from Umberto, and Umberto took her at her word. She'd known him for a year, and had a surreal kind of friendship going with him—or as much as you can make friends with an enemy you knew you might someday have to shoot.

She'd first shown up at the Juarez camp bringing a delivery from a Miami connection, and after a few days she'd mentioned that she wouldn't mind staying. Most of the men had wanted nothing to do with her. They were used to women working in the camp's cantina, not meddling in serious business. Umberto had taken her under his wing and protected her while the meanest of the bunch had challenged her and worked at making every waking minute of her life miserable.

Months passed before her antagonists realized that she'd never quit. If they wanted her gone, they'd have to kill her. Her tenacity eventually earned her some respect. But it was Umberto's protection and Juarez's favor that saved her. Apparently, Juarez had some issues with his Miami connection in the past, and having her leave the man for him pleased the boss on some level.

"How about some *maté?*" Umberto offered. When people met up in the jungle, it was traditional to sit down with a cup of the herbal drink and talk a little.

Would he be suspicious if she said no? She had to take that chance.

"*Gracias,* amigo, but I'd rather get going. Wouldn't mind sleeping in my own bunk tonight." She glanced at Mitch. His facial expression remained neutral, but his tense muscles said the situation didn't please him.

They needed to get back to camp as soon as possible, before he attacked Umberto and the others and put everything, including their lives, in jeopardy. Or kissed her again, God forbid. Her lips were still tingling. What was that about? And did she kiss him back? No way. She'd swooned from hunger and leaned against him for support. That was her story and she was sticking to it.

Umberto gave her an indulgent smile, oblivious to her internal turmoil. "Can't say I don't feel the same. These old bones..." He shook his head, then headed back to the trail with his usual lumbering gait. "*Vamos* then, *chica. Vamos, hombres.*"

Mitch shot her a hard look. He was here on a valid mission, saving a life. She would have helped him if she could have. She didn't want Zak, or anyone else, to come to harm. But more than that, she wanted to save her brother. Zak had to make it back to camp. She wasn't going to sacrifice her brother's life for a spoiled little wannabe drug dealer, no matter what state his father governed.

The kid had been quiet so far, but now he spoke up, stubborn rebellion written all over his face. "No."

"Keep moving." She shoved him forward. He seemed to fail to realize that keeping his head down was the best strategy for him. He didn't grasp the fact that the vast majority of the people present would just as soon shoot him as look at him. Which he proved yet again when he turned to Umberto and said, "Listen, man. I have money."

Umberto laughed as he looked back and gave the kid the once-over, taking in the dirty, torn clothes and sneakers that had seen better days.

"My father is the governor of Kansas."

The few men who spoke English openly laughed at that.

"This man—" Zak pointed at Mitch, fury creeping onto his face "—took money from my father to save me. He was supposed to get me out of here. He betrayed me. Take me home and the money is yours. A million dollars."

Megan shot Mitch a questioning look. *A million?*

But he just rolled his eyes. Okay, so the kid was overestimating his worth. Still, she wondered how big a role money played in Mitch's motives. Was he really more mercenary than soldier? What did she know about the SDDU anyway? Her oldest brother, Jamie, sure didn't answer any of her questions. For a second she wondered how he was coping, how his injury was healing. The worst part of being here was not getting any news about her family back home.

Soon. All she had to do was get out of here alive with Billy.

And at the moment, the key to that was convincing Umberto that everything was fine here so they could hurry back to camp. The man was looking Mitch over carefully.

Mitch didn't even blink. "I think our little boy is homesick." His voice filled with disdain and sarcasm.

Some of the others sneered at Zak.

Umberto turned to Megan. "What disagreement did the boss have with this *chico?*"

She shrugged. "Something to do with business."

"He'll slow us down."

Meaning they should kill him here.

"The idiot shot Enrique on his way out." Megan stepped closer to Zak. "The boss will want him."

The man's gray eyebrows lifted, then he gave a slow nod. "Can't say I ever liked Enrique." He murmured something that sounded like "rabid coyote" and spat onto the ground.

"Forget it, *chico*," he told Zak. "Even if your father was *el presidente* and he offered the White House for you…" He made a dismissing gesture with his hand.

"You have no idea how much money my father has." Zak moved closer, then stopped when Umberto's gun rose. "You could retire."

Megan held her breath, and made sure her hand was close enough to her weapon to draw. From the corner of her eye she saw Mitch positioning himself, too.

Umberto shook his head.

Mitch relaxed and yanked the kid's hands back to tie them at the wrist, holding the end of the rope. "You should have read the career brochure more carefully. There is no retirement from this business."

He kept Zak close. Good. He'd make sure the kid didn't do anything worse than running off at the mouth. If Zak tried to make a run for it, no way could she hold the men back from mowing him down.

Umberto's gaze shifted between them, settling on Mitch. "He's all right?" he asked Megan, his gun still raised.

Her heart rate sped. Juarez would demand Zak, which provided the kid with some protection. Mitch, on the other hand, was expendable. If Umberto wasn't sure Mitch could be trusted, he wouldn't risk it.

Mitch stood still, his stance relaxed, even though he knew his fate was being decided. He gave her a flat smile.

A stone-cold operator would have viewed him as nothing but an obstacle and used this chance to get rid of him. She found she couldn't do it. Not even for her brother.

"I've known him since we were kids," she lied. "I vouch for him."

Umberto lowered his gun at last, then started back down the trail. The men fell in line behind him.

Mitch angled for the last spot in the line.

It gave her a bad feeling. She made sure to walk next to him, keeping Zak in front of them.

"Three days," she whispered under her breath.

Mitch didn't say anything back. His muscles were taut once again, his lips pressed together. She tried not to think about how they'd felt against hers minutes earlier. It didn't matter, because they wouldn't be kissing again.

There was no reason at all why that thought should make her sad, but it did.

They marched on at a comfortable pace, keeping an eye on the jungle, ready for its dangers. They were all seasoned jungle trekkers, save Zak who paid attention to little beyond his own complaining. Soon a breeze picked up, which moved the air around and cleared out the humidity a little. Her stomach growled. She ignored it.

She'd gotten used to going hungry in the past year. Supplies didn't always arrive to the remote camp on time, and Juarez's men weren't particularly skillful at hunting. They could shoot, but they had trouble finding and tracking game. They didn't know the animals well enough to use their habits to help the hunt, couldn't move through the woods nearly as silently as the villagers.

She didn't worry about her hunger. She was just grateful she had enough water. Not that she drank a lot. She wanted to keep bathroom breaks to a minimum, concerned that Mitch might try something if she fell back.

They marched on without taking any breaks. The closer they got to camp, the wider the trail got so at least the going was getting easier. Even so, Zak did slow them down. She and Mitch did their best to nudge the kid along, before Umberto could get impatient.

When the kid stumbled and she reached to hold him up, she bumped into Mitch. They pulled back simultaneously, the tension between them obvious. Good thing they were bringing up the rear, out of sight of the others.

"Three days," she whispered. It was becoming her mantra.

He shook his head.

The rain started up again, a more serious downpour this time.

No sense in stopping to wait. Rain here could go on for days. They were all used to it, and simply put on their hats. Mitch gave his to Zak, then twisted a banana leaf into a handy cone for his own head.

He didn't speak, so she, too, stayed silent as she trekked forward resolutely.

"It's the most logical course of action," she told him when she couldn't stand the silence any longer. Maybe he'd come to see her point and even help her.

But his response ended that fantasy quickly. "This is not over."

MITCH CHECKED OUT Juarez's camp. It had been built on the ruins of an old Jesuit mission. He leaned against the open door of the shed he'd been assigned for the night. He couldn't see much in the dark, but he was familiar with the layout. He'd spent days on recon the first time around, putting together a plan to get Zak out unseen. But before he could have made his well-calculated move, the kid had decided to shoot his way out, messing up everything.

In the middle of the freaking day. Everyone had known what had happened in seconds, and half the camp rushed after them in pursuit.

But only one had caught up with them. Megan.

She was hot as all get-out. He wanted her so badly his teeth ached. Even if she'd messed up his mission in a big way. Even though he might have to hurt her to save Zak. But he didn't want to. She was worth a dozen of the useless kid.

Mitch stretched his legs, his muscles sore from all the miles he'd covered in the last couple of days. The wound on his leg still ached. He watched the night guards to see if their routine had changed since he'd last observed them. It hadn't, it seemed. Good. The next breakout would be done the right way, engineered by him. By the time anyone realized Zak was missing, he and kid would be halfway to the extraction site.

He didn't want to think about where that would leave Megan, but the pesky thought popped into his mind anyway.

He hadn't seen her since they'd arrived a couple of hours earlier.

She'd vouched for him again, even though she had to know that he was just another obstacle in her way. Attaining her goal would have been easier if she let Juarez's men take him out. Or if she'd let Umberto take him out in the first place. But not only did she not turn on him, she didn't speak against him when he'd said he wanted to guard the kid.

None of the other men was keen on sleeping in a drafty shack instead of the cozy bunkhouse. They sure hadn't fought him for the privilege. She had to know this played right into his hands. Yet she didn't betray his true identity.

He hoped she wasn't nursing some dream that he'd help her and sacrifice Zak. If she did, she was going to be seriously disappointed.

Mitch took a look at the kid through the gaps in the shed's wood slats and felt a moment of pity. On arrival, Juarez had punched him in the face hard enough to break his jaw. The kid could no longer talk, which wasn't a bad thing entirely. The less he said the less trouble he would get them all in. He was curled up on his side, worn out and miserable, not even bothering to swat away the little flies that drove every man and woman in the camp crazy.

The trouble with having a permanent camp in the jungle was that every bloodsucker out there learned your address in a hurry and moved right in. Much better to always be on the go, in this one regard at least. Mitch swatted the bugs from his face and thought of the *maté* he'd find in the cantina. The kid looked like he could have used a drink.

But Zak needed something stronger than *maté*. Mitch could afford to walk away for a short while. The shack was padlocked, and Zak wasn't going anywhere anytime soon. Looked like he'd finally hit the proverbial wall. Mitch was familiar with the feeling, as well as the pain of a broken jaw. The key was to compartmentalize the pain and keep going. But he'd been trained to do exactly that, and had plenty of practice. Zak was just a kid. Mitch walked up the path, adding a thin bamboo straw to his shopping list.

He moved in the direction of the most noise. Men were drinking around a bonfire in front of the barracks. He saw no sign of Megan, and wasn't pleased that it was the first thing he noticed. He spotted a bottle of tequila being passed around, grabbed an empty bowl from the ground, and wiped it out with his shirt. Then when the bottle came his way, he sloshed some alcohol into the bowl before passing it on.

Only then did he see Umberto, setting up a line of pebbles, on top of a partially collapsed stone wall. Mitch counted a dozen before Umberto finished and stood aside. Several men lined up fifty feet or so from the wall. Then the shooting contest began.

Mitch glanced toward the shed, ready to return, but two shadows atop the ruins of the old Jesuit mission caught his eye. Juarez's makeshift home leaned against the stone wall, the top of which was used as a lookout. Juarez and Megan were watching the contest from there.

Mitch turned his back to them. Then, without meaning to, he ended up walking toward the lined-up men.

The pudgy bald one at the head of the line hit nine stones out of the twelve. Not bad, considering the darkness of the night and the dancing flames, both of which made judging distances difficult. Umberto put the stones back while the next contestant stepped into position. That one got ten rocks. He moved on after a couple of his buddies slapped him on the back.

Others took their turn. Most of the men were in the same range: nine hits, ten, eleven— clearly people who lived and died by their guns.

"Paolo will hate missing this," one of them called out. "Too bad he's late."

They had no idea just how late. *As in, arrival time: never,* Mitch thought, as he moved to the head of the line. He hesitated. Drawing attention to himself might not be the best idea right now. Still, he couldn't walk away now without drawing even more attention than if he simply took his turn.

He set the bowl at his feet, with half a mind to drink that tequila himself later. Sweat rolled down his temples. The bonfire was too close, the flames licking higher and higher. On the upside, the smoke kept the bugs away. He took off his shirt and mopped his forehead with it, not wanting sweat in his eyes. Then he tossed the shirt next to the bowl. Okay.

One. Two. Three. Four. Five. Six. Seven. Eight. With each successful shot, the men cheered around him, toasting him. *Nine.* A cheer rose again. He looked at the remaining three stones, knowing he should miss.

But then "You go, Mitch!" came from behind him. Megan was cheering for him.

He took out the last three stones with three clean shots in rapid succession, regretting it the second he'd done it. What was he, stupid? Now he was showing off for her?

He should never have kissed her, dammit. Not that he could truly regret that. Those lips… Her body… Her taste… He swallowed a groan.

Maybe keeping him tied up in knots of lust was part of her master plan. Sneaky as the woman was, he wouldn't put it past her.

He glanced toward the wall, caught Juarez saluting him with a glass of something. He nodded in acknowledgment. Then he grabbed the bowl and his shirt and went back to Zak before he could make another stupid mistake.

He didn't need Juarez's attention. He'd be better off flying under the radar so he could get out before anyone had a chance to figure out anything. That was supposed to be his current modus operandi.

Give nobody reason to think too deeply about him. As for himself: think only of the escape. Except his mind was full of questions about whether Megan had been invited up to Juarez's quarters to share more than a good vantage point to watch the target practice. Whether she'd been invited up there to share Juarez's bed.

She was trying to save her brother. He couldn't condemn her. He didn't really care one way or the other, he told himself.

Except, he did.

Damn it all. Damn *her,* in particular. He'd

been thinking… What the hell had he been thinking? Probably whatever she'd wanted him to think.

He was perfectly capable of taking the kid out of the jungle. And yet here he still was.

Megan was the reason, there was no getting around that. First she'd manipulated him, tangling him up in a net of lust. Then she'd probably sleep with Juarez so the man would take her the rest of the way to her goal. The thought ripped at his gut, even as cold fury spread through him, looking for outlet.

At last he reached the shed, and he smashed his fist against the wall, ignoring the splinters that stabbed under his skin.

A frightened moan came from inside.

Mitch pushed the door in, doing his best to banish Megan from his thoughts. "It's me. I brought you something to drink."

MEGAN SNUCK THROUGH the sleeping camp. Zak was back, and other things had gone well for Juarez during her absence, which meant he was happy, which meant the men were happy, which meant they'd drunk even more than usual.

Images of Mitch at the bonfire target practice filled her head—his naked torso glistening in the dancing flames, the way the muscles bunched in his back each time he'd pulled the trigger. She wouldn't have been a woman if she didn't feel anything, if she wasn't the least attracted.

But that was absolutely not the reason why she was sneaking to him in the middle of the night. She had information to share with him.

The night was cool and the bugs were gone until morning, which was a relief. She rounded the barracks and nearly slammed head-on into a dark bulk.

"Chica." Umberto steadied her. "All is well?"

She nodded, looking for an excuse for why she wasn't in her bed, but before she could come up with a semi-logical explanation, Umberto said, "You're going to him."

She didn't say anything. Better to be taken for a fool in lust than a traitor.

"Be careful. I don't like the eyes on that one. That one has secrets."

More than Umberto realized. "We've all done things we don't like to talk about." She shrugged. "I can take care of myself."

"That you can. I taught you well."

He had. She'd learned twice as much about jungle survival from Umberto than from her CIA training. And she had come to like the old guy. He was a murderer like the rest of them. And yet, considering that this was the life he'd been born into, the only one he knew, part of her couldn't blame him. His father had been a bandit, his mother a camp woman, both dead before his first birthday, he'd once told her.

"You're tougher than most men I know," Umberto admitted, then patted her shoulder. "Be careful anyway." He turned and disappeared inside the barracks, before she could have responded.

She moved on, not bothering with stealth after that. Their conversation had drawn the night guard who was walking up the path.

"Que pasa?"

This time, she was ready with her explanation. "Checking on the kid. I worked too hard bringing him in to let him run off again."

"No worries there. I'm on duty." The guard puffed his chest out.

"Pero tu es aqui, mi amigo, thinking about grabbing a bottle from the barracks, while he's all the way over there." She gestured with her head in the direction of the shack and smiled, keeping the mood light.

The guard shrugged, not looking the least

bit concerned. "Your gringo is watching him."

She moved past the man. "I'll do a quick check, all the same."

She strode through the night, toward the small storage building that housed Mitch and the attached shack that imprisoned Zak. She checked on the boy first. He seemed to be sleeping.

She looked up and sighed as the heavens liquefied for the third time that day. Rain drummed on the corrugated metal roof—small, slow drops at first. Then the rainfall picked up, drowning out the jungle sounds that surrounded them.

She went around to Mitch's side, but hesitated. The place had been used for storing weapons before a shipment of them had gone out a month or so ago. She'd managed to stick a tracker on one of the crates. Hopefully the home office didn't have much trouble following it.

She stepped closer to the closed door that was made of a mixture of old boards and bamboo, with plenty of gaps between. Inside, a hammock hung in the corner. It was attached to a hook in the ceiling with a mosquito net draping it. Since no lines from the generators ran all the way out here, an oil lamp on the floor did its best to fill the space with flickering light.

Mitch kneeled in front of a bowl of water on the floor, stripped to the waist, washing up. His physique was more than impressive, more than enough to remind her that she hadn't been with a man in a very long time. Not for lack of opportunity. Plenty had propositioned her here, but they weren't the kind of men she was interested in. Even if she found one among them who wasn't a conscienceless murderer, the moment she'd given in, she would have become so-and-so's woman, and lost all respect and status in the camp. Juarez would never take her seriously then. Which would torpedo her mission. The only thing she should be focused on, night and day.

Yet, she couldn't deny that at the moment she was pretty distracted.

Drops of water ran down Mitch's back, wetting his skin and hair. He looked like some ancient, immortal warrior king.

She swallowed a sudden rush of desire and stepped back, suddenly she was dizzy with need. Better walk away. They could always talk in the morning.

"Come in," he said without turning around.

She stayed still. Okay, so he knew someone was out there. But maybe he didn't know it was her.

"I can smell your perfume."

Shampoo. One of her few small luxuries here. Juarez had summoned her earlier and she'd cleaned up first. Not for him. For herself. She'd been beyond grungy after their trek through the jungle. She wanted to wash the grime off, to feel semi-human again.

She hesitated another long second in front of the closed door, unsure of herself all of a sudden. The attraction that drew her to Mitch was a serious threat to her mission. She didn't like it. She wished they'd met anywhere but here, on any mission but this one.

She found maintaining a professional relationship with him challenging, but since when had she run away from a challenge? She could probably go in there and have a professional conversation without swooning into his arms.

Damn, that was no good.

She drew a deep breath and tried again. She was in control.

"Hey." She pulled the door open and stepped

inside, meaning to leave it open behind her, but it closed by itself on its crooked hinges.

They were alone, enclosed in the intimacy of the small cabin.

Chapter Seven

The air inside was thick with humidity and something else…tension. It infected her immediately, set her on edge, tingled along her skin. The tenuous hold she'd had on remaining calm and collected slipped away.

Mitch shook the water out of his hair and stood. Dark fire burned in his eyes as he gazed at her. His eyes didn't miss a single inch.

She swallowed hard. Maybe coming to him tonight wasn't the best idea she'd ever had.

"I know this is not what you wanted." That was an understatement. He probably rued the day he'd ever met her. "I had no choice but to bring Zak back. My brother…Billy is…" She didn't know how to convince him. Or even if that was possible.

She tried anyway. "When I was nine and we were at my grandparents' farm for the summer, traipsing all over the countryside, I fell into an old well. Billy, Andy and I were playing explorer."

They used to do that a lot. They played explorer, soldier and policeman. She'd had her dolls, but being outside with her eight brothers had always seemed more exciting than combing some boring doll's hair.

"The sun was setting," she went on. "Andy ran for help. Billy climbed down after me, because he knew that even though I would never let on, I was a little scared of spiders. He fell halfway down the well and broke his ankle. I was fine." She shook his head at the memory. "He was five, but such a little hero already."

Mitch watched her, his gaze intent and focused.

"If things were the other way around... Even if I was in the darkest burrow of hell, on the most godforsaken spot on earth, he would come after me."

Seconds ticked by. She had no idea what he thought, what he felt. Awareness grew between them until the tension became unbearable.

It didn't look like she was going to convince him of anything. And if she stayed much longer, she might be the one who caved.

Just give him the news, and get out, she told herself.

"We're leaving for Don Pedro's place at first light," she said quickly. "The trip's been moved up."

"Juarez told you that?" He stalked closer, his shoulders stiff, his gaze never moving from her face for a second. His presence and masculine energy filled the small space.

She nodded. "I got the sense that he was nervous. Toward the end of our conversation, he took a call. I left, but waited outside the door." She prattled on. "From what I could make out, some of the other bosses are coming to the meeting, and he thinks one of them might make a move against Don Pedro. He thinks it's Cristobal." She had no reason to share that information with Mitch. His presence here had nothing to do with the local crime lords, but she didn't seem to be able to stop talking.

"I see you prettied yourself up for him." He stood within arm's reach, his voice cold—a contrast to all the heat in his gaze.

"I spent the last couple of days in the jungle. I was due for a bath."

He stalked closer still, inhaled the air around her.

Blood drummed in her ears, drowning out the rain.

"So he's taking you with him. Congratulations." His voice took on an edge of sarcasm. "How convenient."

She had no idea what he was talking about. She tried to step away from him, but he grabbed her shoulder to hold her in place. He wasn't rough, but firm.

"Have you?" His voice was a coarse whisper as he searched her eyes. The lamplight behind him cast long shadows that obscured his face.

The heat of his palm burned through her thin shirt and sent shivers of awareness down her spine. "Have I what?"

"Been to his bed?" The words came out slowly, as if he was speaking with effort.

Anger rose inside her, and she shoved him. But she might as well have shoved a Kapok tree. "Go to hell."

His eyes glinted dangerously. Instead of letting her go, he moved closer. Then crushed her lips under his.

His kiss was punishing, but her body responded anyway, denied need bubbling to the surface. Then he pulled back, and ran his fingers through his hair in frustration. "Sorry. I—"

"Shut up." She moved forward and pushed her lips back against his.

He took things from there. A myriad of sensations spread through her. Her mind melted as images of Mitch flashed through what little of her brain was still working: the way he'd rushed from that bathroom at the guesthouse, naked, ready to defend her; his wide shoulders hovering above her as he'd torn Paolo off her; the way he'd looked by the bonfire, the quintessential alpha male, winning the shooting contest.

He mastered her mouth the way he mastered everything else. Hesitation wasn't part of the man, in this situation or in any other. His kiss wasn't anything like the unwanted advances of the other men in camp. They'd left her cold and annoyed. She'd left them with a black eye, or worse.

Now desire hit her like a sudden jungle storm and had her drenched in need. Mitch's body, pressed so tightly against her, felt like pure, primal power. It was overwhelming, but being overwhelmed by pleasure didn't seem an altogether bad thing.

"Megan." His voice, raw with desire, got under her skin, coursed through her veins and turned up the heat.

She opened her mouth to him and he deepened the kiss with a low groan that rumbled up his chest and fed straight into her. His lips and tongue possessed hers, conquering her until she was limp, then gently caressing her until she felt her body might fly apart with need.

She couldn't remember the last time, any time, when she'd let her defenses down so completely, had trusted her partner so fully, without reservations. Where had those gone? She'd had plenty of them when they'd first met.

She liked the guy, liked his intelligent chestnut eyes. He was quick and sometimes funny. He was competent. He had principles that ruled his actions. She felt safe with him, which was ridiculous. They weren't more than temporary partners, their goals still mutually exclusive.

They needed to talk about that. Once her brain got back to work. For now, she let him kiss her to his heart's content and hers.

But soon things went beyond that. She *needed* him to kiss her.

Then she needed to kiss him back.

Then she needed to touch him. That was his fault. He shouldn't have been half-naked.

His skin was warm and wet, and her palms glided over his impressive muscles. The nerve endings in her fingertips were singing an ode to joy from the contact.

His hands moved to the underside of her knees and lifted her up in one sure motion, pushing her back against the wall, and wrapping her legs around his waist. His need was unmistakable and gratifying.

She lost her breath when his hardness pressed against her core. A slow ache began somewhere inside her. Her hands caressed his wide shoulders, then moved up to dig into his wiry hair.

Nothing had felt this good in a long time. He didn't try to dominate her, but she knew neither would he yield. They shared some sort of a connection that was undeniable. Maybe because he was the only person in a hundred-mile radius who knew the truth about her, the only one she might be able to trust.

Her breath hitched when he carried her away from the wall and tumbled her into the hammock, which swung precariously in response. A surprised squeak escaped her lips.

"Is this going to work?" She looked up once she tore her lips from his. Could those hooks hold both of them? "I don't think—"

"Watch me." He slipped in adroitly next to her.

The material stretched to accommodate him. For about a second, she was conscious of their perilous position, but then his hand snuck under her tank top. And once his long fingers began massaging their way up her rib cage, she wouldn't have noticed if they crashed to the ground and the roof caved in after them.

She had no idea how he divested her of her light shirt so quickly or how he peeled her out of that tank top, but he did. Then he shifted her so she lay on top of him, her breasts pressing against his bare chest. She'd given up wearing bras a few months back and now was glad for it. The tight straps and the underwire were a nuisance in this heat and humidity. And now...

Now she'd found another advantage.

He gave a sound of primal satisfaction when her nipples rubbed against his chest.

Pleasure zigzagged through her in response. Wow. Double wow. Nobody had ever made her feel like this. Not Vincent, for sure. So unfair that she would have this with someone she shouldn't be anywhere near, someone she might never see again after this night.

But maybe it was better that way. Her circuits were melting, her fuses blowing. Mitch was simply too overwhelming. She'd never have full control of her life with a man like him in it.

He caught her lower lip between his teeth and nipped, then trailed kisses down her neck. Then he pushed her higher, until the soft, wet heat of his mouth could envelop her nipple.

Sure, she'd missed a man's hands on her body. But right now she felt as if it had been Mitch's hands, specifically, that she'd missed all along. A crazy thought.

Her back arched. Her brain stopped functioning.

More heat built inside her with every tug of his lips, with every touch. Her hands explored his hard chest, the rippled muscles of his abdomen. He was built as perfectly as a man could be built. She hesitated at his belt buckle.

His hands slid down to cup her bottom and

press her more tightly against him. He rocked under her. She held on to his hip, trying not to moan too loudly. No sense in alerting the night guard or waking Zak up. Thank God, the rain provided them with some cover.

"Don't think. Feel." His raspy whisper skittered along her nerve endings.

When his mouth switched to the other nipple, she felt the tug between her legs. He moved under her with just the right rhythm. Pressure built. She was going to heaven, but couldn't reach it. Not yet.

He shifted them carefully, pinning her underneath him, and pulled down her cargo pants so his clever fingers could reach the spot where she ached the most. He kissed her deeply and thoroughly as his fingers found a breath-stealing rhythm.

Now. She went for his belt buckle, and fumbled. Her muscles weren't exactly obeying her every command. They were quivering.

Then she couldn't move at all. Those quivering muscles contracted suddenly, held at the edge of the precipice, then tumbled over it as pleasure pulsed through her body in towering waves.

She clung to Mitch's hard body, breathing in hoarse gasps, moaning his name.

Long minutes passed before the ripples quieted. She was beyond sated. Dazed. So it made no sense that she would want more of him, but she did. Deep inside her.

She shifted to wrap her legs around his slim hips. "Take off your pants." Her voice was a breathless whisper she barely recognized.

"We don't have protection." His words came out in a strangled tone.

She blinked. How could she forget that? She'd never forgotten that before, not ever.

"Then let me." She moved to slip her hand under his waistband.

At the same time, they heard Zak groaning on the other side of the wall.

Mitch moved to the side, pulled her next to him and gathered her in his arms. "You're heading out in a couple of hours for a long trek. Rest."

"But—"

"We'll add it to your tab." He smiled at her in the semidarkness. "Someday, somewhere, I'm going to show up in your life and collect."

Suddenly that seemed like a wonderful idea. She kept her hand on his abdomen and rested her head on his shoulder. Idiotically happy, she closed her eyes and breathed in his scent, her body still buzzing with pleasure.

When she fell asleep, her dreams were all about him. Erotic, every single one of them.

Waking in his arms was incredibly nice after all those lonely mornings. And she'd been lonely here, despite all the people in camp. She hadn't made any true connections. For someone who grew up in a family with nine kids, the isolation was pretty difficult to bear. Not that she wouldn't endure much more to save her brother.

Thinking of Billy woke her up the rest of the way, and she felt guilty for indulging in a night of pleasure when her brother was suffering in Don Pedro's dungeons somewhere.

Outside, she heard the team getting ready for the trip. Jeeps were being loaded, four-wheelers roared.

"Time for me to go," she whispered. She needed to refocus, needed distance.

Mitch stirred and pressed against her, his body in the same hard state it'd been when they'd fallen asleep. Maybe he'd been bitten by a banana spider after all.

That reminded her of Zak wanting to see

one. Which reminded her of the rest of the news she hadn't had a chance to tell Mitch.

His warm hand moved up to cup her breast. She placed her own hand on top to still him. If he began to touch her again, they'd never get out of the hammock.

"The guy Zak shot wasn't just Juarez's brother-in-law," she gasped—she was having difficulty breathing as his fingers brushed against her nipple.

Mitch withdrew his hand silently and listened.

"Enrique was also Don Pedro's half brother." It was much easier to talk this way, even if she did miss his touch. "Juarez is under orders to deliver Zak to the Don. The kid is coming with us."

He shoved himself out of the hammock, setting it swinging perilously, and looked at her through narrowed eyes, his demeanor growing colder by the second.

"This is what last night was about." His voice was rigid steel.

The connection that had built between them overnight disappeared. He seemed a thousand miles away. Unreachable.

A sinking feeling spread through her stomach.

"You made sure I didn't go out so I wouldn't hear the news myself. Made sure I was busy so I couldn't break the kid out before you all left in the morning." His chestnut eyes held disappointment and distaste, as if a snake he'd thought harmless had suddenly bitten him.

Denial surged to her lips. "No. Mitch—"

He dragged on his shirt and was out the door the next second, moving as if he couldn't get away from her fast enough.

Chapter Eight

Mitch strode through camp, doing his best to forget the way Megan had come apart in his arms during the night, and denying the fact that every cell in his body still wanted her. He searched for Juarez, but when he found the man, he didn't approach him. Instead, he ambled over to a Jeep nearby where Umberto was struggling with a large crate of supplies.

"You need help?" he offered.

The older man watched him for a long second. Umberto obviously had seen a thing or two and had better instincts about people than most. He hadn't gotten drunk the night before with the others, hadn't participated in any of the fights that later ensued. He shrugged at last. "Sure. *Bueno.*"

So Mitch picked up the nearest bag and tossed it in the back of the Jeep, making sure Juarez saw him. "Has the infamous Paolo returned?" he asked after a few minutes, not bothering to keep his voice down. "Yesterday I heard talk of his legendary shooting skills. Maybe he and I could have a friendly contest someday."

Umberto shook his head. "He's a tough one. If he ain't back, there's a reason." Again, his gaze stayed on Mitch longer than necessary.

From the corner of his eye, Mitch saw Juarez catch their conversation and frown. The boss barked a few quick questions at the man standing next to him. Mitch couldn't hear the low-voiced response, but it seemed scared and apologetic.

He hoisted a crate into the car. Umberto put the jugs of water in place. Between the two of them, the Jeep was packed in ten minutes.

"Gracias," Umberto said as he patted down the bags and jiggled things into place, making sure they were secure.

"De nada, amigo."

Mitch walked back toward his shack, helping whoever he could on the way without making a big deal of it. Megan was gone by the time he reached his quarters. No surprise there.

He could still smell her shampoo. And he could see her glorious breasts rising above him as she'd straddled him in the hammock. His body grew hard all over again.

He swore under his breath and put the memories of the night out of his mind. She'd fooled him again, plain and simple. "But this will be the last time," he swore.

He grabbed his backpack, shoved his handgun into the back of his waistband and left the shed. He checked on Zak through the gaps in the wall. The kid was drinking water through the bamboo straw he'd made him last night.

"You all right?"

"I'll see to it that my father makes you pay for this," Zak hissed through his lips, barely moving his swollen jaw.

He couldn't argue. He'd messed up the moment Megan had walked into that clearing at the river and he'd allowed her to join them. Mitch shook his head and moved on, making sure to pass by Juarez and his men again. He knew one thing only. There was no room for any more mistakes on this mission.

"Adios, then," he called out to Umberto. "Have a good trip."

"Where are you going?" Umberto asked obligingly.

"Thought I'd hunt a little while you guys

are gone." He kept walking, but called over his shoulder. "A camp the size of this one can always use more meat." Hopefully, that would remind them of his shooting skills the night before.

He strode toward the woods. He was almost at the edges of the camp, about to melt into the jungle when a shout rang out.

"Alto!" Stop.

He took two more steps as if not realizing the call was for him.

"Alto! Alto!" One of Juarez's men was running after him.

"What is it?" He turned then, obligingly.

"The boss wants you to come with us. We're shorthanded without Paolo."

"How long a trip? I just got in. Wouldn't mind taking a few days break here in camp."

"You only come to the first drop-off. You guard the goods there and wait for the pickup. You can rest until we come by to get you on the way back."

So the crates and bags in the Jeeps didn't all go to Don Pedro. There'd be some sort of a drop-off of illegal goods in the jungle.

He wasn't trusted enough to be taken all the way to the big boss. Fine. The important thing was, he'd keep sight of Zak for a while longer. They were taking him part of the way, which was better than sneaking after them and trying to track them unseen. If he couldn't get Zak away before that drop-off, Mitch would figure something out so they'd take him farther.

He caught Juarez watching him from a distance, so he made sure he wasn't overenthusiastic as he accepted. The man who'd been sent after him clapped him on the shoulder with a grin anyway.

Mitch didn't return it. He was all business, every bit the mercenary he claimed to be. "So who do I talk to about pay?"

SHE DIDN'T KNOW if she should be impressed or consternated.

She was a CIA agent—she didn't get frustrated easily, Megan reminded herself. Trouble was, that left impressed, and she didn't want to be impressed by Mitch.

Bad enough that she'd been thoroughly seduced by him. While on an undercover op in the middle of an enemy camp. There had to be a whole manual full of rules against that somewhere. Not that she wasn't breaking all the rules already by secretly working to free her brother.

The two Jeeps followed each other closely

on the narrow, bumpy road, followed by three ATVs. It was much easier than going on foot, even if the logging road was no more than a collection of potholes in the muddy soil. She was afraid that by the time they reached their destination, the journey might shake her teeth loose.

Mitch was avoiding her on purpose. He'd chosen to ride in the other car, and he never came anywhere near her whenever they hit a particularly bad patch of road and had to get out to help the cars over.

Each time, he worked harder and longer than anyone, earning some of the men's grudging respect, and the resentment of others who didn't like Juarez's approving eye on him. He brushed that off, just went along with the lifting and the pushing.

She knew the game he was playing. According to Umberto, Mitch was to stay at the drop-off site and rejoin the team on their way back. The drop-off was tonight. Mitch wanted to stay with the group longer so he'd have more time to rescue Zak.

And mess up her plans.

She'd vouched for him, back when she'd still hoped he would come around to help her. If he did anything stupid, it would be her butt on the line. Juarez would assume they were working together. He'd shoot first, ask questions later.

She would have liked to think that Mitch wouldn't do that to her. But as mad as he'd been at her this morning…He was convinced she was the enemy.

If Mitch took off with Zak… Even if she managed to convince Juarez that she wasn't in cahoots with him— She'd been the one who'd brought Zak back the first time. If the kid disappeared again, and by some miracle, Juarez didn't blame her, he'd send her after Zak for sure.

Except, she didn't have time to chase after the kid again. She needed to go to Don Pedro at any cost.

So her primary focus at the moment was to watch Mitch like a hawk and make sure he didn't spirit Zak away when no one was looking.

When their convoy came to a small creek lined with moss-covered stones, she jumped to the mud to lighten the load. So did most of the others.

"It's slippery," the driver said. "Water's higher than last week."

They'd had plenty of rain since then. Megan

walked alongside the car as they crossed, in position to help if the current began pushing the vehicle downstream. Cold water filled her boots. At least she had dry socks in her backpack so she could change into them when they reached the other side. Walking around with wet feet in the jungle was asking for trouble.

Using her femininity as an excuse to stay in the car didn't even occur to her. Her continued survival depended on the men knowing that she was as tough as they were. Tougher.

They reached the other side fine, but climbing ashore turned out to be more difficult than the crossing. The mud was deeper here. The lighter ATVs made it up the bank fine, but the tires of the two Jeeps got stuck, which meant another round of heaving and dragging.

If she hadn't been watching Mitch so closely, she wouldn't have noticed that this time, instead of helping, he sneaked away into the jungle.

"Need a drain," he called back with a grin.

Except none of the men ever walked very far to relieve themselves. But Mitch went far enough that she could no longer see him at all.

She moved closer to Zak, trying to figure out Mitch's game.

He was back in ten minutes. And he was walking funny.

Maybe he'd pulled his back lifting the Jeep and walked off so the men wouldn't notice his pain. Maybe he just didn't want to seem weak. Since he didn't go anywhere near Zak, Megan relaxed and went back to work, focusing her full strength on what she was doing.

Then they were done at last, muddy, cold and exhausted. A short break was ordered. They'd build a fire so that everyone could dry up and grab a bite to eat.

Mitch sat next to Zak, talked to the kid under his breath while the others loudly joked around. They hoped Don Pedro had gotten new women to do the cooking. They hadn't fancied the last batch of cooks who were old enough to be their mothers.

Megan shook her head good-naturedly at the comments. She rolled her eyes at the more raunchy jokes, but watched Mitch every chance she got, making sure she was close enough to stop him if he made a move. She didn't like this sudden cozying up to Zak. As good as Mitch was… She didn't dare turn her back on him for a second.

He was not going to mess up her plans.

She strode right up to Juarez as soon as her bowl was empty. "The kid's riding with me. Got some questions for him about how he escaped. I don't like it that a kid like this got through our security."

Juarez shrugged, busy with his meal. He liked his food and it showed on his midriff. He no longer went on long marches through the jungle; he had plenty of men for that. If he needed to see to something personally, he took one of the Jeeps.

He was getting comfortable in other ways, too. He'd simply had the guard who'd let Zak escape beaten. A year ago, when Megan had shown up, gross negligence like that would have been punished by a shot to the head.

There'd been two previous trips to see Don Pedro since Megan had been at camp. No matter what she'd done, she couldn't get on Juarez to take her along. She'd been told she needed to earn his trust. Yet Mitch had easily managed to get himself invited. Only to the halfway drop-off point, but still. Juarez was relaxing the rules.

That didn't bode well for him, especially if he was right and one of the other captains was planning an internal war. Juarez had been doing too well for too long, and he was getting cocky.

Megan grabbed Zak by the elbow and dragged him to the second car so they could ride together. When she glanced back at Mitch, she expected him to be angry. Instead, a look of satisfaction sat on the man's face, which he quickly masked.

She had no idea what that was about. Didn't matter. Zak was hers.

"What did he tell you?" she asked the kid.

"To keep my head down so I don't get into any more trouble."

She watched Zak's face for telltale signs that he was lying, but didn't see any. "Try to remember that."

They piled into the cars and took off, but didn't get far before the first Jeep veered off the road and nearly crashed into a tree. Everyone jumped out of the car, swearing up a storm.

Everyone, except Mitch. His knife flashed just before something brownish-green flew from the vehicle. A snake.

A second passed before she recognized the shape of the snake's head. It was a fer-de-lance, a spearhead. A shiver ran down her back.

"Stay," she ordered Zak, as she jumped out to take a closer look.

The men had already gathered around the snake. Four feet long and still wriggling—the deadliest snake around. In this jungle, spearheads were responsible for more deaths than any other animal.

There wasn't a face that didn't go a little pale. She felt the blood draining out of her own.

Juarez shook off the scare first.

His gaze settled on Megan. "I owe you my thanks. This man you brought to us is a good one. He saved my life today."

Mitch.

Oh, man. She'd left Zak alone in the car and every man's attention was on the snake. Except for Mitch's, and he wasn't here.

She whipped around, expecting both him and the kid to be gone, but Mitch was right behind her. He stepped forward, bent and cut the dead snake's head off with a clean swipe of his knife, speared it on a stick and held it out to Juarez.

Juarez took it and grinned at the open mouth, at the fangs. It was the exact kind of trophy he liked, although she had no idea how Mitch would know that.

The other men who'd been riding up front seemed equally happy with their latest comrade in arms, but Umberto, who'd been driving the Jeep Megan and Zak rode in, narrowed his small brown eyes as he watched the proceedings.

Looked like Mitch's sudden rise into the boss's favor was gaining him at least one enemy. Odd, since Umberto was one of the most easygoing of the men, not given to fits of temper or jealousy. Still, Mitch would be smart to watch his back, she thought as she headed back to the car and the kid.

Part of her wanted to warn Mitch about Umberto, but doing it without anyone hearing didn't seem possible at the moment. And Mitch wasn't talking to her anyway. He was just going to have to handle any trouble he got himself into. Her first priority was her brother.

Several hours passed before they reached the drop-off point. They unloaded one of the Jeeps. From the feel of the bags, she was pretty sure the load was drugs and not weapons. She couldn't find a way to tag these bags without being seen, so she tagged a nearby tree, sticking a micro transmitter onto the bark when she leaned against it for a minute of rest. That way, her CIA team would be able to find the drop-off location.

The sun dipped lower and lower. They needed to get their camp ready. She helped where she could and stayed out of the way otherwise. She needed to stick to Zak who was unusually subdued, nursing his jaw and looking beat down and miserable.

She cooked, even though she never did that in camp, leaving kitchen work to the cantina women. But now she was the only woman at hand and traditional gender roles lived on in the jungle. She didn't mind. At least she knew what she was eating. Some of the men were less than discerning when it came to food out here. She dropped dried fish into the filtered water and let it boil, adding cleaned roots and native herbs they'd brought, supplemented with a few that she found near the clearing.

While the others ate, she spoon-fed some soup to Zak. "You need to eat some of this, even if it hurts."

She made sure he had enough water and his straw, even brought him a cup of *maté* later and helped him drink it. He was in bad shape, but he could have been in worse. He could have been dead by now. She sure hoped he'd learned his lesson. And if Mitch managed to get him home in one piece, she prayed he would do something useful with his life.

"You take the second car for the night," Juarez called across the fire to her.

To be given the car to sleep in was a treat. Juarez was probably rewarding her for bringing Zak back and for adding another good man to the boss's team.

"With the kid," he added. "He better still be here come morning."

No problem there. She'd already planned on tying the kid to her wrist with her boot laces that night.

The drop-off point, where they'd set up camp for the night, was at loggers' crossroads. Collapsed sleeping platforms were visible here and there where loggers of the past had rested. Umberto was repairing one. The rest of the men made new ones for themselves.

Megan helped Zak to another drink, but she became distracted when she heard the sound of an enraged shout.

Mitch and Umberto were facing off. Umberto cursed him with all the color of the Spanish language. Something about Mitch bumping into him and spilling his drink. "Watch where you're going, gringo!"

Mitch stood his ground, darkness gathering in his eyes. Umberto moved closer and put the honor of Mitch's mother in question. A muscle ticked in Mitch's face. More insults were shouted about gringos and all the cowards who lived in the U.S. of A. He was provoking Mitch, taunting him until he couldn't take anymore and moved toward Umberto at last, rolling over him like a tank.

Umberto was older, but he was also taller than Mitch, and had grown up fighting. He'd made his living with his fists all his life. He had moves that weren't taught at any law enforcement academy, and a familiarity with jungle terrain that no one could match.

The men gathered around and cheered, not a thought given to pulling the battling enemies apart. They thought this prime entertainment, business as usual. Fights were frequent at the camp.

Megan watched Mitch, her hands curled into fists.

The stupid idiot. She could have punched him herself, given half a chance. Did he have a death wish? Umberto might have been the closest thing she had to a friend at camp, but he was a hardened criminal. She never allowed herself to forget that.

If Mitch got injured… A broken rib could be a death sentence out here. Two months back, after a fight like this, a broken rib had punctured a man's lung. He died before he could reach the witch doctor in the nearest village.

Her jaw tightened. She was not going to worry about Mitch, she told herself. He deserved whatever he got. But she couldn't look away, either.

The men rolled on the uneven ground, too near the fire. Umberto grabbed Mitch's collar from the back and pulled hard, trying to cut off his air. But the fabric gave instead, ripping down his back. Then Mitch was on top, pinning Umberto.

He waited, sweat rolling down his neck, until the older man capitulated. Then he stood, letting Umberto go with a cocky sneer. Which was too much for the proud Umberto, who went on the attack once again.

Mitch bent deftly out of the way, barely bumping his opponent who fell face-first into the fire. Umberto pulled back howling.

"Enough!" Juarez ordered at last, and

others stepped between the fighters to separate them.

"I didn't mean for him to get hurt." Mitch submitted to the boss immediately, apologetic. Then he turned to Umberto. "Sorry, amigo." He wiped his forehead. "It's this damned heat."

"You let him go. He came back for more." Juarez let Mitch off the hook even as he scowled at both men. The boss watched as Umberto poured water over his burned face, hissing.

Megan grabbed her jar of salve and ran to help, shooting an angry glance at Mitch as she passed.

"Let me look at that," she told Umberto. "It's not that bad. You'll heal. Anyway, women like a man with battle scars," she said, trying to make Umberto feel better.

"Something about that one isn't right," the man told her under his breath. He was holding up pretty well considering the pain he must be in. "You watch him, *chica,* or he'll burn you, too. You'll see. You keep an eye on him."

"Te lo prometo." I promise.

Juarez kicked one of the bags that held supplies, displeasure written all over his face.

"Umberto will stay with the goods. The gringo is coming with us in the morning," he declared before he stalked away.

Mitch shrugged, not seeming to care one way or the other, not looking pleased with his victory. He glanced at Umberto. "You all right?"

Umberto swore at him in Spanish and told him to drop dead.

As Mitch shuffled off, suspicion swirled through Megan. He'd wanted to come with them to the end, and now he was coming.

Convenient.

Had the fight been engineered? Maybe he hadn't spilled Umberto's drink by accident. He'd sure gained Juarez's favor in a hurry, something that had taken her nearly a full year to do. Granted, the fact that she was a woman had counted against her in a big way. The most difficult part of her job had been to overcome that.

Then she thought about the snake, the way Mitch had gone off to the woods and come back walking funny. Even he wouldn't have hidden a poisonous snake under his clothing, would he? No. She decided against it. Nobody would be that crazy.

Yet, if she'd learned anything since she'd

met him, it was that he would do anything to achieve his goal. He would stop at nothing to complete his mission and get Zak back home. On a professional level, she appreciated that.

She'd have appreciated it even more than if they were partners. But they were clearly working at cross-purposes, which meant she had to watch him 24/7.

If it came down to a choice between saving her brother or Zak, Mitch would save Zak. A fact she would do well to remember.

She made sure their paths crossed when he started down to the creek for water. "So you're coming with us to the meeting," she remarked, watching him closely. His face didn't betray a thing.

He filled his canteen then took hers and filled that, too, so she didn't have to stand too close to the muddy creek and get her boots wet. She glanced around to make sure there was nobody within hearing distance.

"Billy always liked the jungle," she said as she looked up at the tall trees that seemed to reach the sky. "He was excited when he found out that his assignment would bring him here."

"And you? Was this what you wanted?"

She gave a sour laugh. "When I first signed

up…I was thinking more plush European jobs. I'd have loved to go to Paris, in particular. Do a little shopping, a little intelligence gathering, that sort of thing."

He handed her canteen back.

"The first week of training pretty much killed most of my TV-inspired fantasies," she admitted. "Billy tried to talk me out of the job, actually. Before I signed up, and a couple of times after. He worried that I'd get into trouble somewhere far from home. And then he did."

Mitch stomped the mud off his shoes and began walking away.

"He has a girl back home, Amy. She's a kindergarten teacher. She's just the sweetest thing."

Mitch didn't wait for her to catch up. He didn't seem to be interested in her, or stories of her little brother. He was a man on a mission.

Well, she was a woman on a mission. And she wasn't done fighting.

Chapter Nine

Mitch ambled around Don Pedro's compound, hoping to catch a glimpse of Zak. He'd been carried off the moment they'd arrived at the meeting point, and hadn't been seen since.

He should have taken the kid before they'd gotten this far. He'd thought about it several times during the night at their makeshift camp in the jungle, then again during the long trek that had brought them here. Yet he hadn't acted.

Something had stopped him, and if he wanted to be honest, he had to admit—at least to himself—that something was Megan. He wanted her to be able to save her brother. Even if she'd used him. If he was going to catch any flak for that from the Colonel, he would just have to deal with it.

The jumble of structures that made up the compound didn't seem to have been built according to any logical plan. It didn't seem possible that law enforcement hadn't discovered the place. The two-acre clearing in the jungle had to be clearly visible from the air. On top of the largest building, a two-story Spanish-style house complete with a balcony; there was even a helipad. A chopper was parked there at the moment.

Juarez's camp—with its roughly made wooden shacks—had an air of impermanence. He camped like a man who knew he might have to disappear at any moment, putting as little work as possible into the place, and spending as little money on it as possible.

Here, only half of the dozen buildings were the traditional wooden abodes with palm frond thatching that were native to the area. The rest were made from brick and cement. Every building had power—the hum of generators filled the air. The lights were on behind almost every window and more were strung between the buildings, holding back the night.

A semi-decent road led to the compound's gate, the only entry through the barbed wire fence that guarded the perimeter to keep out the wild animals. Mitch didn't think the *polizia* ever came here, unless it was to pick up bribes. From the sweet setup, it sure looked like Don Pedro had friends in high places who provided him with protection against such inconveniences as police raids.

"Tequila, amigo?" A man who could barely stand propped himself against a building and waved his bottle at Mitch.

"No thanks. I'm good for now, I think." He gave a friendly laugh as he moved on.

The place buzzed with people, crowded with all the newcomers. Juarez wasn't the only visitor. At least four other captains had come with their posses, from what Mitch had been able to overhear. Cristobal was among them. A mean one, from the looks of him.

His eyes said he'd shoot you if you so much as sneezed. A heavyset man, but not in the way Juarez was. Cristobal had the build and demeanor of a prize fighter. His face was scarred, his nose crooked—it must have been broken in the past. Mitch had caught a glimpse of the man when the captains had gone up to the Don's big house together.

He headed toward the cantina, nodded to the men already there, but didn't join any of their conversations or arguments. Didn't say anything but *"Gracias,"* when a quarter bottle of homemade tequila was offered to him. He settled on a log in the corner, his back resting against the rough-hewn wood of the wall, his eyes half-closed, the very picture of a man exhausted by the long trip.

He listened. Also, he kept an eye out for Megan, but didn't see her. She was probably looking for her brother.

The talk centered on guns and women. Nobody was talking about Zak, or where any prisoners might be kept. After half an hour, Mitch slipped away. A useful clue could have saved him considerable time, but from the way the conversation had gone, sticking around would just have been a waste of time.

He shouldn't have let the kid out of his sight. But Juarez had wanted him to help unload the Jeeps, and there was no way to refuse the boss without arousing suspicion. And by the time Juarez had been done with him, the kid had disappeared into one of the buildings.

Except, he was no longer there. Mitch had checked that building first, the moment he'd been able to get away. He didn't find any bloodstains on the floor, at least, which gave him hope that the kid was still alive. They'd just moved him when Mitch hadn't been looking.

Don Pedro was busy this evening receiving his captains, who'd probably give him reports on their activities and his cut of the cash from all the shady businesses they ran. But the grace period wasn't likely to last beyond morning. Tonight, the men ate and drank. They would do that long into the night, at the rate they were going. But in the morning, they would remember Zak, the man who'd shot the Don's half brother. Then there would be a reckoning.

Mitch had until then to get the kid away from here. That was all the time Megan had, too. When Mitch disappeared with Zak, her close association with him would get her into trouble. She couldn't afford to linger. He hoped she was making headway.

He stopped to adjust his left boot, glancing around surreptitiously to make sure no one was watching him. Then he ducked into a narrow space between two buildings.

Nobody called out after him.

He moved quickly, looking for entry into either building. Eventually he found a padlocked door on the right. It took him less than two minutes to get in.

The lights were out, but enough moonlight came in through a row of windows that he could see the half dozen long tables that lined the walls. And scales, wrapping materials, all the paraphernalia of a serious drug operation.

He glanced up at a narrow walkway suspended from the roof beams. When the workers were getting these packages ready, a couple of armed guards probably stood up there, making sure nobody stole anything, making sure there was no trouble.

He walked around, checked every shadowed corner, knowing if Zak was tied up in here somewhere, he might not be in good enough shape to call out for help, even if the kid did see him in the semi-darkness.

A ten-minute search turned up no sign of him. No sign of Megan's brother, either. Zak was his priority, but if he found Billy, if the man was still alive, he would help Megan. He might not have had a brother, but he did have Cindy, a sister he would have killed or died for.

He understood where Megan was coming from. Understood it and respected it. That was why he was still here, instead of already cutting through the jungle on his way back home with Zak.

It didn't have anything to do with the way his heart stumbled every time he looked at

Megan Cassidy. Definitely not. That would be stupid.

He eased back out the way he'd come in and snapped the padlock closed behind him.

"Que pasa, gringo?"

The voice made him spin. Juarez. The meeting with Don Pedro must be over.

Mitch made a point of craning his neck around. "I thought I saw a woman come in here." He put a confused look on his face as he came forward from between the buildings, making himself sway on his feet. "I swear the *mujer* disappeared into nothing." He blinked hard. "What do they put into the tequila around here, anyway?"

The boss laughed at him. "A *mujer,* eh? Come with me."

He hesitated for a second, calculating how quickly he could grab his knife and sink it into the man's heart, how quickly he could drag him into the shadows of the narrow space.

Quickly enough, if there weren't any others around. But a handful of men played a dice game in the dust in front of the building opposite them and, alerted by Juarez's voice, they kept looking his way.

He joined Juarez with a forced grin. "Lead the way."

Half an hour went to waste before he could get away again, leaving one relieved woman behind. With all the strangers in camp and all the drinking, the women had plenty of requests and were plenty tired. The woman Juarez had introduced him to hadn't taken offense when he'd changed his mind. He even got an affectionate pat on the back. Judging by the noises coming from the loft above the stables that housed the packing mules, Juarez was oblivious to anything but his own satisfaction.

Mitch checked the stables on his way out, and found two more couples who were taking advantage of the soft hay, but no sign of Zak or Billy.

He ducked out the door, heading for another building he hadn't checked yet. The main house, the one with the balcony and the helipad on the roof, he was leaving for last. Don Pedro's private quarters had to be well guarded. His chances of getting caught would be the highest there.

He snuck into the barracks, and found them mostly empty, save for the few men who'd drunk themselves unconscious and had somehow dragged themselves back here to crash. In the darkness, he stumbled over a boot someone had left in the middle of the room.

"Hey, *chica.* Come here," one of the drunks called from his bunk, his words followed by a hiccup.

Mitch moved on without response, shaking his head. He worked his way back to the narrow alley where Juarez had almost caught him, and rounded the building he hadn't been able to get into before. It was dark inside. At last he came to a door in the back.

He wiggled the doorknob. Unlocked. He stepped into the darkness, closing the door quietly behind him. He knew at once that he wasn't alone. Tension hung thick in the air.

"What do you want?" The barked Spanish words came from the far end of the room. People moved in the darkness. "Turn on the light."

Not a chance. He wasn't about to make himself a target. He ducked low and readied his gun.

Someone groaned. Two muffled shots were fired. As if the barrel of the gun was pressed into something that dampened the sound, like a body. *Not Zak,* Mitch thought. Zak would be called to task in front of the Don, made an example. Not Billy, either. If Megan was right, they'd had Billy for a year now. Why execute him suddenly and in secret?

He opened the door at his back and rolled out of the building a second before a bullet shattered the door frame. This one would be heard. He dashed into the bushes behind the building and laid low. Three men rushed out, but they only looked for him for a few seconds before taking off. They knew the gunshot would bring the Don's guards.

Sure enough, shouts rose in the camp. Mitch couldn't move without being seen. But if they found him here… He couldn't afford to be held and questioned. As the night wore on, Zak was running out of time.

He couldn't slip into the jungle, either. The fence was at his back. He was trapped.

MEGAN HAD BEEN HIDING behind the cantina for at least twenty minutes when the gunshot sounded and all the men she was watching ran off in that direction. Hopefully, Mitch wasn't in trouble. She shouldn't have cared as much as she did. Of course, she shouldn't have slept with him, either. There was something about him that made her break rules she'd never broken before, something that put that funny fluttering in the middle of her chest.

But it wasn't anything she could stop and contemplate at the moment.

When the area cleared at last, she headed for a double padlocked door in the back, which she thought might lead to her brother. No other place she'd checked so far held any clues. She prayed to God this would be it.

She picked the lock and stepped inside the dark space. Her senses told her she was in a small room. Wood planks squeaked under her feet as she stepped forward tentatively. Her heart beat faster.

Every cell of her body was alive and alert. After a year of planning and jockeying for Juarez's attention, she had finally made it, she was here. Billy had to be somewhere nearby. This was it. She grinned into the darkness, then reminded herself not to get too carried away on the rising tide of hope. She needed to keep her focus, now more than ever.

She moved forward by feel, bumping into a soft, solid mass that could have been a dead body, but turned out to be a sack of something. Her hands, held out in front of her, grazed jars. Glass clinked in the darkness. She felt a shelf. She was in the pantry. Well, all right. Logical for a room built right into the side of the cantina.

She didn't dare turn on the light, so she lit a match and looked around carefully to make sure she didn't miss any hidden doors or crawl spaces where a prisoner could be stashed.

She saw nothing. No way out of the pantry except the way she'd come in. Disappointment tightened her throat as the match went out. She only let the feeling touch her for a second. She shook off all negativity before she exited.

A couple of drunks were singing about love and war in the distance. Didn't hit a single note between them. She cringed as she snuck in the opposite direction. She had one more building to check before she moved on to the main house, the most well-protected place in the compound.

Everything she saw she cataloged, every crate of guns she found she tagged, every word she overheard she remembered. She was still a CIA operative and planned on filing a report when she got back to the office. She hoped that would make up for her gross breach of conduct here at least a little.

She made a note of the helicopter on the

roof up ahead. She hadn't flown one in years, but in a pinch… She snuck toward another cement building that was a quarter of the size of the main one. This one had a double lock instead of a padlock. Her hopes rose. They must keep something important here.

But as her heart raced, she heard the sound of a few men approaching, and pulled herself into the shadows.

"Then what the hell was the shot about?"

"Guard said he couldn't find anything."

"Probably Jose got drunk again and couldn't help showing off his new pistol to his buddies."

"The man could never hold his liquor. He's worse than a woman." The speaker spat into the dust as his friends laughed in agreement.

She didn't move back to the door until they were well away. She pulled her set of picks from her back pocket. But before she could put them into the lock, the door opened. The building wasn't dark—the windows had just been blacked out from inside, she realized, too late.

"Chica." An immediate grin spread on the man's pockmarked face as he looked her over. "I saw you earlier." He lifted a bottle toward her. "You want to go someplace for a drink?"

He was better dressed and more well-spoken than most of the others. He probably had a higher position in the organization, which didn't impress Megan.

"No thanks. I like to stop while I can still stand."

"A woman with principles." The man nodded. "Can't find many of those in the jungle." He watched her thoughtfully for a second. "You belong to Juarez?"

"Gotta have a protector in this business." She shrugged.

"True enough." The man looked her over again, this time with regret. "You better find your man before you get into trouble. The boys had too much to drink tonight. They see a pretty girl… They aren't thinking."

"I was just looking for him."

"He's not in here." The man locked the door behind him, then took off for the barracks without a backward glance.

She moved on, circling around the building. When a large cloud covered the moon, she tried the front door again. The double lock was tricky to pick, but not impossible. Then she was in, the door closed behind her.

Since the windows were blacked out, not a smidgen of light filtered in from the outside.

She reached for the light switch, but couldn't find it. Some of the small buildings she'd been in had pull switches that hung from a light in the middle of the room. This place probably had the same. She moved forward.

Then a small noise made her freeze.

She held her breath, listening.

She didn't hear another sound, yet every instinct she had screamed that someone was moving toward her. The short hairs at her nape stood on end. She pulled her knife. The gun would make too much noise and draw an audience.

She backed away slowly, silently, until her back bumped into the wall. Pulse beating, she waited.

No attack came.

The silence continued until she thought she might have just imagined the noise earlier. But no, she definitely felt a presence.

She turned toward the door. She would come back later.

A solid wall of flesh blocked her way. She bit her lip hard to keep from screaming. Then steel arms came around her to restrain her, knocking the knife from her hand.

"It's me," Mitch whispered into her ear just as she brought up her elbow to launch an attack.

"Was that necessary?" She smacked him on the chest, both angry at him and relieved beyond words. Something inside pushed her to lean against him. She checked that impulse and didn't give in to it.

"I didn't know who you were until you came close enough that I could smell your shampoo."

He made that up. She hadn't washed her hair since they'd been at Juarez's camp. No way he could still smell that.

"How did you get in?" She moved away from him in the darkness. Maybe a little distance would stop her from being so aware of his body.

"Back window, while you were chatting up your guy up front."

"He's not my guy," she snapped, annoyed with the situation, and the fact that she still hadn't found Billy. "Did you find anything?"

"Two extra rooms in the back. All locked up tight." His sexy voice skittered along her skin.

"Been inside yet?"

"I was about to see to the locks when you interrupted me. Careful." He took her hand and led the way back through the darkness. "Where have you been?"

She shouldn't have enjoyed his touch so much. They weren't holding hands in a romantic way. He'd already been across the room and knew the path, leading her only to make sure she wouldn't bump into anything and give them away.

Knowing that didn't stop heat spreading across her skin, however. She tried not to think of his hands on other places on her body, but she failed. The night she'd spent in his hammock refused to be forgotten.

Focus on Billy.

"I've checked everywhere but here and the main house. Did you have anything to do with that gunshot?"

"No, but I was there. Would have gotten caught, too, if not for a hole in the fence." He lit a match so they could see the lock.

There was a hole in the fence. Good to know. "What was it about?"

"Not sure. Could be Cristobal is making his move. Or private business between the Don's men? Could be about drugs or a woman."

They reached the door and he let go of her hand.

She immediately missed his touch. "The Don's men were shooting at each other?"

"I couldn't see well enough to tell."

She thought for a second. "I caught a glimpse of the Don a couple of times, before they locked themselves up in the main house. He was definitely keeping a close eye on Cristobal."

"All the more reason for us to get moving and get the hell out of here."

She couldn't agree more. She shoved her picks into the lock and worked the tumblers, then pushed the door in.

They found themselves in small private quarters. There was a bed, a table, some shelves.

Mitch even checked under the bed. He pulled out a dusty duffel bag. He claimed that, fingering something on the bottom, hesitating before tossing in some dry food, plus a box of matches. "Something for the trek out of the jungle."

Good thinking. Neither of them had their backpacks. She figured walking around camp with her gear would draw attention. She'd written it off as a loss. Once she found and grabbed her brother, they would be out of here. There'd be no time to go back for anything then. Mitch must have thought the same.

He looked at the last locked door left before

them. "Zak and Billy are either here or at the main house."

Hope expanded in her heart. Her fingers were trembling so this time she held the match and Mitch saw to the lock. Her hands never shook. Ever. At least, not until now. But this time was personal.

She understood, at last, why the agency didn't let its operatives get involved in missions where they had a personal stake. Everything *was* different. At least she had Mitch with her.

He opened the lock in no time. No surprise there. He seemed to be good at everything.

"Put the match out," he said as soon as he stepped inside.

She blew out the flame, frustrated that he knew what was in the small room but she hadn't seen anything. "What is it?" Was somebody coming? She listened for footsteps.

"Explosives storage."

Given a choice, she would have preferred not to go in there. But something scraped at the front door of the building. Then they heard voices.

Mitch yanked her into the dark room and closed the door behind them.

They flattened themselves against the wall,

one on each side, and waited. She had her knife drawn, plus her gun handy, in case everything went to hell. *Please, God, don't let it end here. Let me find Billy.*

Three men came in, judging by the voices. They complained about the food in a mixture of Spanish and some local language. There hadn't been quite enough to eat, the soup was watered down.

"We'll go hunting in the morning," one of them offered a solution. "We'll make a fire right in the forest and have a full meal. To hell with the visitors."

"The Don said nobody leaves while the visitors are here," another responded.

This was followed by some long and colorful swearing.

She heard a familiar beep a few seconds later. Someone had powered on a computer out there. Anything was possible with a generator, she supposed. The main section of this building must be some sort of office. Long minutes passed by. The men talked now and then, but they weren't leaving. At least they weren't coming into the storage room, either.

Once their door rattled, setting Megan's nerves on edge. In a few minutes, the sound of snoring reached her. Someone must have hunkered down right in front of the door for a nap.

After a few tense seconds, Mitch pulled away and sat on the floor. She sat next to him, careful not to bump into any boxes in the dark.

"Are we stuck?" She kept her voice low, although the man snored loud enough outside to drown out her words.

"I'll figure something out. Give me a second."

Someone turned a radio on outside. Salsa music filled the air, which meant they could talk a little without being heard.

"Billy will be mad that I came. I might be older, but he always thinks women should be protected. When I was fourteen, I got home from my first date with a guy and he got fresh with me in the driveway. Billy dropped out of our tree house like a ninja and attacked him. He was ten."

"You don't have to do that anymore."

"Do what?"

"Tell stories about your brother to make him into a real person in my mind so I'll go along with your plans and help."

He didn't miss much. At least, he no longer seemed to be mad at her.

"Looks like they're in the main house," she whispered after a moment. "Billy and Zak. That's the only place left. We could bust them out together." She went for the logical solution. The two of them together would make a pretty good team. Not that she would ever acknowledge that she was asking for Mitch's help.

"That's the plan."

His announcement gave her pause. "It is?" *Since when?*

Then something occurred to her, certain events of the past day making a little more sense. "Is that why you didn't take off with Zak in the woods when you set up the great snake distraction?"

"You've vouched for me with Juarez," he said with some reluctance.

"But keeping me alive isn't your mission. Taking Zak home is." She winced. That sure sounded like she was arguing against herself. Better shut up while she was ahead.

"We'll do this together."

His voice was steady, like the man himself. Her heart turned over in her chest. She'd set out to do this alone. She'd thought she preferred it that way. The fewer people involved, the fewer chances for mistakes.

But Mitch was… The truth was she was lucky to have Mitch by her side for this, and she knew it.

"The night before last, in your hammock, that wasn't a ploy on my part. I had no intention… I went there to tell you about the change of plans."

Silence stretched between them.

"All right," he said after a minute.

Some of the tightness relaxed in her shoulders.

He shifted toward her. "I need you to answer a question for me. Honestly."

Considering who she worked for, she couldn't promise that. "Ask, and I'll see what I can do."

"How do you know Colonel Wilson?"

She hesitated for a second. "I met him a year and a half ago."

"Where?"

"At my mother's house. He came to visit my brother."

"Billy?"

"Jamie."

Another moment of silence. Then Mitch swore softly under his breath. "You're Jamie Cassidy's sister?"

"Didn't I just say that?"

"So this Billy is Jamie's little brother?"

She grinned in the dark. "We're all siblings. Do you want me to draw you a map?"

"Why didn't you tell me sooner?"

"Do you know Jamie?"

A full minute ticked by before he answered. "By name only. We're connected through…um…"

"You both work for Colonel Wilson." It annoyed her to death that she knew so little about her brother's work. If Jamie didn't want to talk about something, you couldn't get a word out of him with bloody torture. He'd been like that even when they'd been kids.

"I'm sorry, ma'am, but I can neither confirm nor deny that," Mitch mocked her, acting just like her infuriating brother.

"The Colonel came to visit Jamie after he got out of the hospital." He'd lost both legs on a mission he wasn't allowed to talk about, and she hadn't been able to uncover anything despite all her CIA connections.

"I heard he's had a rough time of it."

She couldn't talk about that. The way Jamie had been the last time she'd seen him… It had broken her heart. And the worst part was, there was nothing she could do to help. But she could help Billy. Nothing was going to happen to Billy. Not as long as she was alive and her heart was beating in her chest.

"We should get moving."

For a second, Mitch said nothing, and she was afraid he was going to push her about Jamie, but when he did speak, he said, "Let's give the guys out there a little time. It'd be better if they cleared out on their own. I'd rather get out of here quietly than draw attention to ourselves."

"How long do you want to wait?" Impatience pushed her forward.

"Half an hour. If they don't move on by then, we'll find a way to take care of them."

"And until then?"

"We could both use some rest." He brushed against her back as he lay down. "Once we bust Billy and Zak out, we'll have to get moving fast. It'll be a while before we can stop to take a break."

She lay down next to him. "So what do you know about my brother?" She needed another picture of Jamie, different from the last time she'd seen him in that wheelchair with the light gone from his eyes.

"Jamie Cassidy is a living legend. He's saved the lives of hundreds. If the mission he'd been on could be acknowledged in any way, he'd be receiving the Congressional Medal of Honor."

She swallowed hard, thinking of Jamie, struggling to accept the loss of his legs, the loss of his spirit. If Jamie were well, he would be here. If Jamie were well, he would have already gotten Billy back. But now she was here to do that. And she'd get it done no matter what.

"Thanks," she told Mitch. "Thank you for telling me. It helps."

Colonel Wilson hadn't been able to tell her family anything when he'd visited, just that they should be proud of Jamie. The man had talked with her brother for two hours behind closed doors before he'd left their house. Man, she'd been steamed. Tears pricked her eyes now. She missed Jamie. Not knowing how he was doing had been the most difficult part of the past year. She missed all her brothers.

She didn't even think of resisting when Mitch pulled her into his arms. She felt a new connection form between them as she relaxed against him.

He ran his fingers down her hair. He must have read her subdued mood, because he said, "We're almost there now. It's almost over. We'll do this as a team."

"Good," she said with sincere relief. "You were a pain as an enemy."

He gave a low chuckle. "Right back at you, darling."

"I've been waiting for so long to be this close. It seems surreal. Until now, all I worried about was making it this far. Now that I'm here…" Suddenly she thought of a million brand new things to worry about.

"There's nothing we can't handle together."

His voice held warmth and comfort and strength, so she asked the question she hadn't dared ask even herself until now. "You think Billy is still alive?"

"If he's anything like you or Jamie, they couldn't take him out with a bazooka."

That put a smile on her face. And then, all of a sudden, those stupid tears spilled over and ran down her cheeks. She rubbed them away with the heel of her hand, but more came. Great. Just great. So much for her tough-chick image.

She didn't cry. Ever. She'd lost that annoying habit growing up. Having to duke it out with eight brothers on a daily basis taught her to never show weakness. They teased her mercilessly if she so much as slowed down because of a scraped knee or busted finger.

Mitch brushed the pad of his thumb along her face, right through the streaks of moisture.

Wonderful. Now he knew that she was a complete mess.

But he didn't tease her or laugh at her. He kissed her.

Chapter Ten

Another man might have told himself he was only kissing Megan to distract her from their troubles, but Mitch had always employed brutal honesty when it came to women. They confused him enough without game playing, so he never lied to them, or to himself.

He wasn't tasting Megan's lips like he was a starving man to comfort her. He was doing it because he wanted to. Because he wanted her.

"We'll get them out. Don't worry about it. I don't leave men behind. Not ever," he whispered against her mouth.

She burrowed against him and he folded his arms around her, wanting to protect even though he knew she hated that, that she didn't need protection. She was the most self-sufficient woman he'd ever met. She'd survived a year in a jungle camp with dozens of hardened criminals. That said something about her. She was nobody's damsel in distress.

He went back for another taste of her soft lips.

He wouldn't have minded if she needed him a little. He didn't have much to offer a woman beyond his protection. He couldn't offer a fancy house or a steady relationship, or pretty words. He'd always been awkward around women, and wasn't exactly the play-boy type.

She tasted like mango. She tended to go for fruit during meals, and he couldn't blame her. Cantina fare wasn't exactly haute cuisine. Every meal that came out of those blackened pots was a raffle ticket to dysentery or food poisoning.

The sweet mango taste of her was intoxi-cating. He'd never thought that a taste could go straight to a man's head, but it did. For the rest of his life, mango would be his favorite food, he was pretty sure.

He drank her in, holding on to control. He didn't want to go too far. Or too fast. She wasn't like the other women he had run into over the years, not that there were many. He'd been working special ops at the beginning, in military units where women weren't allowed.

Even now, in the SDDU, they were the exception to the rule. And since most missions were lone-wolf ops, it wasn't as if he got to hang out with them all that often.

He didn't have many opportunities to hone his seduction skills. For most of his adult life, he'd been busy fighting for his country. So being here now with Megan, trying to negotiate the rules of their cooperation, while trying to negotiate the rules of their attraction, was new to him.

They broke apart for air. She shifted slightly away. Now she would tell him that this was a big mistake, he thought, a protest all ready on his lips. But instead she whispered a question.

"Did you once leave someone important to you behind? Is that why you make sure that won't ever happen again? Was it a woman?"

She'd been thinking about that? He was definitely clueless about women. Did their brains never stop?

He let her go and rubbed his hand over his face. The one he'd left behind…

He didn't want to go there. Not ever. But maybe because of the darkness—or more likely because of Megan—the words poured out from a cold, locked-away part of him.

"My mother is an alcoholic, the mean kind. My father is a drug addict. I had a sister, Cindy. She was much younger than me." Fifteen years, to be exact. "When Cindy was about a year old, my father sold her for drugs." A vast emptiness opened up inside his chest, a cold place where only his nightmares lived.

She moved closer and leaned her head on his shoulder.

"My father was too out of it to remember where he took her or who he gave her to. I ran away from home to look for her. But I never found her. The police never had a clue, either." He put his arms around her and held her tight. "I've never given up, but…God, it's been twenty years."

She pressed her lips to the side of his stubbled cheek, and he drank in the comfort. Inside his heart, a couple of barricades crumbled.

"So this is why getting Zak home is a religion to you, no matter what a twit the kid is, no matter how I'd begged. I get it." She moved her head and lined up her lips with his. Didn't kiss him. Just left their mouths touching like that.

The gesture was sweet and erotic at the

same time, just like the woman. And the thing was, he really did believe that she understood him.

He pressed closer and deepened the kiss. She gave him everything.

Long minutes passed as their passion heated to a fever pitch. He ran his hands over her back and arms, not sure what to do next. This was the time when women wanted to hear something romantic. He wished he were better at this. *Go with the truth.* "I don't want to stop."

She stilled.

Great. Why couldn't he have thought up something sweet?

But the next second she pressed closer to him, making his body harder in an instant. "I don't want you to stop, either."

The thrill of that simple sentence shot right through him. He cupped her breasts as arousal, gratitude and other, more complicated, emotions swirled inside him.

This was dangerous, he thought. He knew this woman. Wouldn't easily forget her. He cared about her. When did that happen? Didn't matter, he supposed. It was the bare truth.

So don't mess it up. He didn't intend to.

He planned on stopping way before the point of no return. He just wanted another feel of her amazing breasts. Just one more second to soak up the sensation as they pressed into his palms.

Her hand slipped under his shirt and rested against his abdomen. Her slim fingers drove him to distraction. She moved up to his chest, and as she ran her palm over his nipple, he sucked in a sharp breath.

When she began unbuttoning his shirt, he did nothing to stop her. He'd been shirtless with her before. They weren't going too far. Yet.

His hands moved reluctantly to give her room to maneuver and ended up at the hem of her tank top. He hesitated. She moved back a little and arched her back to help him. He pulled up the stretchy material inch by slow inch, taking her unbuttoned shirt with it, pulling it all over her head.

His eyes were used to the dark enough now to see the outline of her perfect breasts. The thin line of light coming in under the door helped, too, and he was more grateful for that little light than he'd been for anything in a long time. Her nipples were swollen and ready, and drew his lips like magnets.

He didn't even try to resist. He could have been happy like this, alternating between her breasts and mouth, for the rest of his life, he thought. Then her head dropped back, her back arched and her hand slipped down between his pants and his skin.

All of a sudden, he didn't have enough air to breathe.

His body flexed against hers. Those slim fingers wrapped around him.

This would be a good time to stop.

He was glad to know that a few of his brain cells were still working. Part of his brain remained alert to their surroundings and the danger around them, listening for the men outside, making sure the one in front of the door kept snoring. The rest of his brain had drowned in testosterone and need.

No. He couldn't let that happen. That would be irresponsible.

"We're going to stop now," he said.

"No," she told him. Her fingers tightened around him in emphasis.

Okay, not yet. She was right. They were still in control. They could wait a little and stop later.

Her scent and the feel of her filled him completely. When she undid his belt buckle for better access, he lost his breath. She was a whiz with the zipper. She was a whiz with pretty much everything, so he shouldn't have been surprised.

His most impatient body part sprang free. His pants, halfway down his thighs now, limited his movement. In the cramped storage room, they couldn't lie down and stretch out comfortably. He felt as if they were playing some erotic version of Twister.

He went for her pants and tugged them down, wanting to make her feel as good as she made him feel. With one hand on her breast, and another between her legs, he turned her and backed her up until she sat on his lap, with him kneeling behind her.

His hard need nestled against the smooth skin of her backside, the exquisite sensation filling him up with steam. She leaned her head back to rest it on his shoulder, offering her neck to his lips. At the same time, she rubbed her bottom against him.

"We can't," he begged on a raspy whisper. She was pushing him beyond his limits. But they *could*. The duffel bag he'd fished from under the bed in the other room hid a little present.

He had left the package of condoms on

the bottom of the bag because they could be useful on their way out of the jungle. Condoms could keep an injury protected if they had to cross a river. They could also be used to collect water. They were elastic enough to make a sling out of for hunting, if he ran out of bullets. Condoms had enough uses, that they were a standard part of survivor kits.

"Right." She drew a slow, shuddering breath and lifted her head from his shoulder, leaning away from him. "This is beyond idiotic. I don't know what I was thinking."

"Don't apologize." His voice held a low rasp that hadn't been there before. He quietly cleared his throat. "You're an amazing woman. I—" What? He couldn't help himself? He hated jerks who said things like that.

A real man could always help himself, always made sure his woman was safe, that he did what was best for her.

Not that Megan Cassidy was his woman.

He wanted to put some distance between them, but he didn't seem to be able to let her go. His arms wouldn't release her.

He pressed a kiss to her nape, but instead of letting her go when he was done, he ended up scraping his teeth along her skin.

She trembled, swallowing a moan before it had a chance to become fully audible.

"Mitch?" The heat in her voice proved to be his undoing.

"I want to." He didn't breathe. "Tell me to go to hell."

Instead, she slid back for more full body contact. His eyes crossed. He didn't care. She had her back to him and it was dark. He didn't have to worry about looking attractive. Or even sane. Which he obviously wasn't just now.

He reached for the condom. "I found something in the other room," he whispered.

She probably figured out what when she heard the crinkling sound of the packaging rip, because she made a noise that could only be described as grateful relief. She lifted away to give him room.

He sheathed himself, still not fully able to believe that they were going to do this. Now. Here.

"Your brother Jamie is going to shoot a hole in my head the size of a railroad tunnel when he finds out I touched his sister," he said, half hoping that saying it out loud might knock some sense into him at the last second.

It didn't.

"Might as well make it worth all the grief he's going to give us," Megan suggested practically.

The next second she was lowering herself onto his hardness.

He gripped her hips, stopped her when he was pressed against her entrance.

There was still time…

Then there wasn't.

His body moved forward on its own accord, and he slid into her wet heat, slowly, to give her time to adjust.

If the room exploded at the moment, he would have died a happy man. And that was saying something, because he would have left his mission incomplete, and he didn't believe in that kind of thing.

She felt amazing. Perfect. Hot. Every move she made blew his mind, until his entire focus was narrowed to the friction between their bodies.

Pressure built. Tension escalated.

"Mitch," she breathed his name a second before her inner muscles began convulsing around him, pushing him over the edge.

All he saw was white heat. All he could hear was his own heartbeat drumming inside his ears.

How did I get so lucky? he thought, as he held her tight, waiting for their heart rates to calm.

A shuffling sound in front of the door interrupted their bliss. "Did you hear that noise?" a surly voice asked.

The men had turned off the radio. The snoring had stopped.

Mitch went for his weapon. Megan moved, too, then stilled again, took his hand and pulled it forward, pressed it to the floor near her knee. He felt some kind of a latch.

It could be a latch door to a crawlspace below the building. He ran his finger around the edges, looking for a handhold.

It was nailed down.

She slid off his lap. He missed her immediately, but had no time to pause and think about that or what they'd done had meant.

His knife was in his hand already, and he pried up the two large nails with the tip. He felt for the edges of the door, opened it, tossed the duffel bag down and lowered himself without even pulling up his pants all the way.

The doorknob wiggled.

He reached up and guided Megan down.

She pulled the trapdoor closed behind her as she tumbled on top of him.

THEY CROUCHED NEXT TO each other silently. Megan's whole body tingled. She could still feel Mitch's hands on her skin. Back there, what'd happened... Nobody had ever... She'd never felt... Wow.

She blinked hard, trying to refocus on their current situation. Moonlight shone through a gap in the wood boards that edged the crawl-space to the right. Beyond that, everything else was shrouded in darkness. Neither of them moved. Not yet.

"Probably rats again," a man said above them. "Can't get rid of the stupid vermin for nothin'. How many times did I tell you idiots not to bring any food back here?"

Then she heard the door close.

Mitch rustled next to her, probably working his pants up. She'd done that before she'd slipped down after him. Now she dragged on her shirt, trying not to think about all the poisonous snakes, spiders, bugs and plants that might be all around them.

She shifted toward the light. Mitch's hand shot out and held her back. He went first, taking on most of the danger.

Her brain still buzzed with pleasure. Her

heart tickled as she took in his wide shoulders, silhouetted in front of her.

He was protecting her.

She hated when he did that. Still, she found it difficult to work up any indignation when she was still boneless from the mind-blowing sex they'd just had.

She drew a slow breath and nearly gagged when she caught a foul stench in the air. Something had crawled in here and died. That pretty much killed the last lingering remains of any romantic mood.

Thank God. Because she really needed to be fully present right now.

"Breathe through your mouth," he whispered back some advice. "Are you all right?"

"Fine." So much better than fine, really. But now was not the time to get into that.

So what if he was taking over for a little while?

She'd always been the protector. The oldest kid in the family. She'd always been her mother's helper, kept her little brothers clean and fed, bandaged their scrapes when they were younger. Kept them safe, which had been a full-time job, with the amazing amount of trouble they'd always managed to find.

Then when they didn't need her quite so much—she'd found a job where she could keep other people safe.

Except, now her family needed her again. Although he wouldn't admit it, though he'd pushed her away and kept the whole family at arm's length, Jamie needed her support. And Billy needed her more than ever.

"Let's go," she whispered, just as boots crunched outside. A couple of men stopped right next to the building.

She froze and held her breath. So did Mitch. Any noise they made would be heard by the men. She wasn't going to make a mistake now. Not when she was this close to reaching Billy.

Chapter Eleven

Megan could hear water running. The air still stunk, this time with the sharp smell of ammonia. Gross. Somebody was relieving himself on the other side of the wooden boards that closed in the crawlspace where they were hiding. Just great.

Her nerves hummed. Mitch put a steadying hand on her knee as if sensing her inner turmoil.

His warm palm heated her skin through the material of her pants. A comforting gesture that also brought back thoughts of what had just happened between them in that storage room.

Her breathing grew erratic. She made an effort to calm it.

If there'd ever been a time when she needed her full focus, this was it. She couldn't afford distractions and complications. But then why did it feel so good to have Mitch on her side?

Whoever was outside finished his business and walked away. After a minute, Mitch began moving. He made it to the opening, climbed out, but continued to crouch. She waited until he gave the all clear.

He was brushing spiderwebs from his clothes when she finally joined him.

She did the same. Yuck. She'd been living in the jungle long enough not to be scared of bugs, but she didn't have to like it. "Anything bite you?"

"I don't think so. You?" He moved forward, constantly scanning their surroundings.

She shook her head as she glanced back toward the narrow hole they'd climbed through. "I definitely wouldn't want to do that twice."

"You need a break?" He slowed.

"I need to find Billy." She kept on going.

They snuck forward, keeping close to the shadows, until they reached a spot where stacks of firewood covered the ground in front of them. The main building stood straight ahead, outlined against the sky. Only three of the windows were lit on their side. It looked like the party had ended. The Don was probably settling in for the night. Or maybe he was already sleeping and the light had been left on for his in-house guards.

"Let's hope Billy and Zak are in there," she said as she followed Mitch, since once again he'd taken the lead.

"They have to be. Don't worry about anything now. We're here."

They rounded all the firewood and stopped in the cover of the last stack. The guards by the house didn't look like they'd over-imbibed like the rest. They seemed alert and up to the task. And well-armed. The security was definitely heavier than at Juarez's camp, and for a moment Megan wondered if this was standard procedure, or if the Don felt uneasy about the presence of his captains at the compound and had tightened security for his own protection.

"Any ideas?" she whispered to Mitch.

"Let's do a walk-around first." He stole forward, sticking to the shadows, of which there were plenty. Trees and shacks crowded Don Pedro's headquarters.

The guard at the front of the house stood by a small fire that burned in a rusted steel drum. More for the smoke that kept the bugs away than for the heat, Megan suspected. The guard watching the side of the house was smoking a cigar and looking bored. The man in the back leaned against the wall to watch the jungle.

Mitch moved quietly in the cover of some bushes. She followed him, noticing a small window low to the ground. Not enough to let anyone in, or out, just enough for some light and air. The main house had a basement.

She tugged Mitch's sleeve and pointed. He acknowledged her with a nod. They checked out the fourth guard who was cleaning his weapon, then crept back to the back of the building.

"Is there any way we could get in through that window?" Her instincts said, if there were any prisoners in the house, they were kept in that basement.

"Not without some serious tools and a lot of noise. The wall is solid cement."

Which meant they had to find another way to get in and out. One of the guards would have to be eliminated. Except shooting him would draw the others. A knife between the ribs would have been much quieter, but for that they would have to get close without being seen, which would be difficult since they'd be out in the open.

"Poison dart?" A few months ago, she'd accompanied Umberto and a small team to one of the local villages and she'd seen a couple of old men hunt with them. A silent and effective weapon if one knew how to use it. Desperation had her considering every option, no matter how far-fetched.

"We could make the pipe and the dart, but do we have time to hunt around for the right frog to get the poison from?"

No. They would never find one in the dark jungle. "If we waited until daylight…"

"We have to make our move tonight. Zak's hours are numbered. Don Pedro has no reason to keep the kid around. We have to work with the assumption that he'll be executed first thing in the morning."

Couldn't argue with that logic. From what she'd seen of the way Juarez operated, enemies were dealt with swiftly in the jungle. Zak wasn't her favorite person, but she didn't want him dead, and she knew Mitch was set on his course. The breakout had to be tonight. Billy's, too, then, since once Mitch rescued Zak, the camp would be in an uproar. They had to do this together.

She drew a slow breath, trying to get her thoughts in order. She'd never been this frazzled on a mission before. She'd never worked with stakes this high. This was personal. Her brother's life was on the line.

Focus. She'd never had to remind herself to do that before. But now distractions surrounded her. Thoughts of her brother. Mitch's presence. Yet she appreciated that Mitch was with her more and more with every passing minute.

He really did make a good partner. He made a fabulous lover, too, but she didn't want to think about that just now. Someday, when they were all safely away from here, maybe they would talk about what was going on between them. It felt like something.

Especially when he caught her hand and held it gently. "Promise me one thing."

She raised an eyebrow. If he wanted her to stay behind and provide cover… No way. Billy was in there. She was going in.

"Promise me you won't get hurt," he said instead.

He cared. Her heart melted a little.

She cared about him, too. More than she would ever admit. That was a straight highway to heartache. They might never see each other again once their missions here were over. "I'll try my best," she whispered. "If you do the same."

She wanted to kiss him. Instead, she pulled her hand from his and refocused on the task. She stared at the back wall of the house, as if looking at it long enough would enable her to see through it.

"Look up," he whispered into her ear after a minute, his warm breath tickling her skin.

She did. A Kapok tree stood near them with a bunch of lianas, jungle vines, hanging in every direction.

Her brain caught up with his in half a second. "You think we can Tarzan it?"

He grinned and they crawled backward, straightening only when they reached the taller bushes that surrounded the Kapok. Then he gave her a boost up the tree.

Climbing in the dark wasn't the easiest thing she'd ever done. She did her best to watch out for tarantulas and snakes, hoping their luck held out a little longer. She bit her lip when her foot slipped. But Mitch braced her bottom, and she didn't fall. She ignored the tingles his touch sent through her and got back to business, balancing on a side branch when she reached the right height.

Mitch inched out onto the tree limb behind her and began testing lianas that hung from above, picked one that didn't reach all the way to the ground, but was long enough to reach the roof. "What do you think?"

When she nodded, he tested the thing, putting his weight on it little by little. It held.

She moved forward to add her weight, but he held her back.

"We're not going together."

Of course not, he wanted to go first. She glared at him in the dark, but didn't say anything. They both had a thing for protecting others. She got it.

He kissed her, hot and hard, before he swung, leaving her startled and swooning. She barely heard him land lightly onto the roof.

The guard didn't even look up.

Mitch tossed the liana back.

She grabbed it and swung without hesitation. He caught her silently, lowered her onto the roof. Held her for a second as the liana swung back to the tree. They couldn't tie it to the roof for their exit. The guard could look up at the sky at any time, see it and realize that something was amiss.

They stood still for a second, pressed against each other. Awareness buzzed along her nerve endings. She wanted a kiss. From the look in his eyes, so did he.

They had a lot to do first. She slipped to her feet and inched away from him, careful not to make any noise. They kept low as they moved along the roof, looking for a way in. The balcony in the front she thought, just as Mitch turned to head that way.

The compound had quieted by this point. Even the cantina, which they could see from up here, looked deserted. Strings of lights lit up the main walkways, the bare bulbs surrounded by clouds of bugs. Some of the generators had been turned off as people had gone to bed, so the constant hum was quieter than it had been earlier, but it was still loud enough to drown out most of the jungle noises. Outside the compound, the woods were dark and ominous. Predators hunted in the night, sneaking around with deadly intent, just as she and Mitch were doing.

They stopped once the balcony was directly below them. The windows were dark. This time, she went first. He held her hands and lowered her until her feet touched the railing. She made her way down from there on her own. He followed her, swiftly and silently.

The balcony door stood open, allowing them entry to a room with a large table and a couple of ostentatious, overstuffed couches. They moved quickly, keeping to the shadows with their backs to the wall.

The door at the other end of the room was locked, but between the two of them, they solved that problem in a minute. The hallway outside led in two directions, with a steep set of curving stairs to the right. The lights were on here. They communicated with hand signals, then moved toward the stairs.

She'd expected to see guards in the house, but didn't. She snuck downstairs first, while Mitch covered her from above. Then she covered him while he caught up with her. They crossed the waiting area at the foot of the stairs. Saw the shadow of the guard outside through the glass in the front door, and took care not to make a sound.

The first room they came across was Don Pedro's private kitchen. He ate better fare than his men, judging by the stocked shelves. Mitch pilfered a few cans as he passed through. They would come in handy on their way out of the jungle.

Down the hall, the sound of snoring came from behind closed doors. The house servants most likely, or Don Pedro's personal bodyguards who were housed in the main building with him. It looked like they weren't required to stand guard at night.

They left that room alone. The next door revealed a bathroom. Now *that* was luxury in a place like this.

The only door left stood at the end of the corridor. A solid wood door that looked at least three inches thick, with a good lock. They had to spend more time on that than on any of the other locks they'd come across so far. When they were done, they opened the door which revealed a staircase in front of them that led down into darkness.

They had no way to tell whether a guard was on duty with the prisoners. Once Mitch closed the door behind them, they could see little, so they silently took each step with care, pausing at the bottom of the stairs.

Something moved in the back of the room. They froze, aiming their weapons blindly.

"Is Roberto down here?" she asked in Spanish, as she pushed Mitch behind the cover of the staircase. She could protect him, too. If a guard slept down here, she would just pretend that she was looking for someone named Roberto, in hopes of a quick roll in the hay. "He said he was coming up to the house."

Roberto was a common name. And even if there wasn't one among the house guards and servants, whoever was down here couldn't know if there wasn't a horny Roberto among the visitors.

"Megan?" Zak's voice came out of the darkness, somewhere to her left, the single word mumbled. His jaw must hurt like hell.

"Sis?" another voice asked.

Billy.

She stumbled blindly forward, her heart beating out an erratic rhythm in her throat as she fumbled to light a match. She had to try three times before she managed.

"Anyone else down here?" She peered into the darkness, saw a hole in the wall and headed that way.

A cell. They'd kept him in a dank cell all this time. Part of her rejoiced over finding Billy, another part was furious at the bastards who'd treated her brother like this.

"Just me and another guy. He's hurt. Is that really you?" Billy's voice came from the hole.

Mitch lit a match, too. They didn't dare risk turning on the lights. The guards outside would see it through the small windows.

A hairy face appeared in the hole in the wall. She recognized the eyes first. She stuck her hand in without hesitation, and the next second her fingertips were touching Billy's. A tremor ran through her, tears burning her eyes.

Her brother was alive. He was here. Sure she'd believed in that for the past year, but blind faith and physical proof weren't one and the same. Her throat tightened. A long second passed before she could talk again.

"I'm taking you home. Hang in there. Are you okay?"

"Meg." Regret mixed with excitement in her brother's voice. "It's too dangerous. You shouldn't have come." A deep, shuddering breath. "Oh, man. I can't believe you're here. I figured everyone would assume I was dead by now."

She wanted to lean her forehead against the wall and cry. But they didn't have time for such luxuries.

"Let me see the door." She let his fingertips go with reluctance and moved along the wall toward the door. Then she lit another match.

"Don't touch it. The alarm goes off if I so much as lean against the damn thing."

"Mine, too," Zak said from the other side of the basement, pushing the words out with effort. He needed medical care for that jaw as soon as possible.

She examined the wiring of the alarm. What the hell? Now she knew why Don Pedro didn't think a guard was necessary down here.

She could hear Mitch swearing under his breath as he checked Zak's door, but her full attention was on her brother. The alarm system was some sort of a homemade job, with no logic to it whatsoever. Wires, wires and more wires, all in a jumble. Her experience would mean little here. This would take more than a few minutes, maybe more than a few hours.

"I'm not giving up now," she promised Billy, wracking her brain for a solution.

"Who else is with you?"

She didn't like how weak his voice was. "A friend."

"Just one?"

How to explain Mitch? "He's like Jamie."

"He's got no legs?"

"Funny to the last," she murmured, barely able to understand how Billy could still joke after what he must have endured during the past year here. Then again, he probably wouldn't have survived if he'd lost his sense of humor.

"It's too late, sis," he whispered through the door.

Like hell it was. "I'm here to rescue you now," she promised. "Don't you worry about anything."

Mitch came over. "Can't do a damn thing about that alarm. Everything okay here?"

"We'll figure it out. How is Zak?"

"He'll make it. I think we're going to have to blow our way out."

Having her brother within arm's reach at last, she was so overwhelmed, she could barely think. "What are you talking about?"

"You can't get into their explosives stash." That came from Billy. "They guard it 24/7. I got that far before. They caught me when I tried to steal some of the good stuff to blow the compound up as a parting gift."

Knowing that he'd actually gotten out and had been captured again twisted Megan's heart. This time, the escape would be final. She thought of the trapdoor to the crawl space below Don Pedro's explosive storage.

"We've got our own VIP entrance. Don't you worry." She reached in through the hole again and squeezed Billy's hand before she turned to leave. Time was of the essence. In less than two hours it would be morning. Don

Pedro's men would be waking up and going about their business, making sneaking around a lot more difficult. Not to mention that they would be coming for Zak in short order.

The four of them better be gone long before that.

"All we have to do," she thought out loud, organizing the action, "is sneak out unseen, steal an armful of explosives, then sneak back in. We'll blow out the cell doors then blow a hole in the back wall that's closest to the jungle. We'll be gone before the dust settles."

"Piece of cake," Mitch said with a chuckle.

The basement was too dark for her to see his face, but she was sure there would be a glint in his eyes. The man wasn't scared of anything.

"No," Billy said from behind the wall, putting force into his voice. "You sneak out, get away from this place and don't come back here. Meg? Please."

"I'm not leaving without you." She'd come here for him. She'd planned this moment for over a year, went to bed and woke up in the morning thinking about how she could do it.

"I've been in this tiny cell for too long. I'm sick, sis. I'm weak. I can't make it out of the jungle."

She didn't want to hear it. "Then we'll carry you on our backs."

Mitch checked the basement walls with the help of another match, looking for a good spot to put the charges. She trusted him to get it right.

"I don't want you to get hurt because of me." Billy's voice filled with frustration. "Meg—"

"I'm taking you with me." They were not going to have a discussion over this. No way.

"What's left of me… I'll be no use to anyone ever again, sis. There's no point."

"I'll be the judge of that." She knew this mood, the dark heaviness that came through Billy's voice. Jamie had sounded the same the last time she'd seen him. Well, she wasn't going to let either of her brothers go out like that. They might have given up, but she was still fighting. "You just get ready."

"Meg—"

"Don't be stupid. I didn't come all this way to leave you here."

It was just like Billy to argue about his own rescue. He'd been always like that. Headstrong. Never willing to take anything at face value, never accepting her advice just because she was oldest and knew better.

"You know how much I hate it when people fight me when I'm doing something for their own good." She tried to lighten the mood. They could all use a little of that.

He gave a sour laugh. "God, it's good to see you again. I didn't think I'd get the chance. I'm grateful for that, sis. More grateful than I can ever say."

"You two can do the family thing once we get out of here." Mitch grabbed her by the elbow and tugged her toward the staircase. "Time is running out here."

"Don't waste any of it on me." Billy stayed stubborn. "If you want to get something out, get out Don Pedro's game book. It's worth a hell of lot more than I am."

"What game book?" Mitch slowed and turned.

"He's got a book where he keeps track of all his passwords to his online accounts, the location of his goods, that kind of thing. He's got a laptop, too, but he's paranoid about somebody hacking it. He keeps the most important information on paper. I overheard one of the guards talking about it a couple of months ago."

Billy coughed, and she didn't like the sound of it. But before she could ask if he was all right, he continued. "It's in his office. In his safe."

"I'll try," Mitch said. "We'll be back in half an hour. Be ready," he added.

"Does it have to be explosives?" Zak protested, but his jaw kept him from getting too loud. "What if you make a mistake and kill me?" He kept on going despite the pain each word must have caused him. "My father is rich. I can negotiate with people here. They won't turn down a bag of money."

Mitch ignored the kid and walked away, muttering something under his breath that sounded like "Too bad money can't buy brains."

They needed half an hour to get the explosives and get back into the building. Possibly another half an hour to set everything up. Safe and effective demolition took a lot of careful prep work. It was right on the top of the list of things that didn't pay to do in a hurry.

They'd be cutting it pretty close, Megan thought as she followed Mitch up the stairs. She hoped Don Pedro's men weren't early risers.

Chapter Twelve

Mitch stopped at the top of the basement stairs and ran through their options. His original exit plan had been to grab Zak and Billy, then shoot their way out through the front door. The jungle was just steps away behind the house. They could sprint along the fence to the hole he'd found earlier, and disappear before most of the drunken camp woke up, got dressed, grabbed their guns and came around to see what all the noise was about.

Except he didn't have Zak and Billy as he'd planned. They had to come back for those two, so they couldn't make any noise on their way out, couldn't be discovered.

"Back to the roof," he whispered to Megan. The liana was gone, they couldn't leave the way they'd come, but another plan began forming in his brain.

They snuck down the hall, a pair of moving shadows stealing up the main stairs. But when they reached the top floor, he didn't head for the balcony or the nearest window.

The game book wasn't part of his mission, but he was here, steps from it. Wouldn't have made any sense leaving it behind. He'd lost too many good friends to people like Don Pedro. If he could take one crime lord down, he was more than willing to go a few steps out of his way to do it.

Megan followed without asking any questions. She'd probably guessed what he was doing, had probably been planning on doing the same thing. Their minds worked the same way in certain regards. It made them a good team.

He could see five doors on this level. One was to the living room with the balcony where they'd come in. One of the other four had to lead to the study. He was holding his knife instead of his gun. If he needed to take anyone out, he'd do it silently.

He tried one door, Megan tried another. They silently opened them just enough to see inside. Enough moonlight came in through the windows to see the basics.

A bathroom. He glanced back at Megan and shook his head. She shook her head back at him.

They crept forward.

He put his hand on the next doorknob, heard a snort from inside. A bed squeaked as whoever occupied it turned. Don Pedro, probably. He tried the knob. Locked.

Mitch looked at the last door, the only one they hadn't checked. It had a keypad entry. This one was a professional job, standard security. Don Pedro had been willing to spend money here, unlike on the rigged-up job on the basement prison. Ironically, that was the door's weakness. Mitch knew just about every standard security unit inside out. Outsmarting this one only took a few minutes.

Then he and Megan slipped into the office together. He closed the door behind them, scanned the room in the moonlight. "Where's the safe?"

The desk was a plain top with four legs. No drawers. The few shelves in the room mostly held guns. There weren't any pictures on the wall to hide a wall safe. He circled the room along the wall anyway, looking for any irregularities.

Nothing.

"The floor," Megan said and flipped over the carpet.

Nothing there, either.

Maybe Billy didn't have the right information.

None of the furniture in the room looked large enough to hide a safe. Nothing on the wall or floor indicated a hiding spot.

"The bookcase." Megan strode that way.

He helped her push the carved wood bookcase aside, along with the small rug it had sat on. And there was the safe, an old, manual one, not electric, built into the floor. Don Pedro probably wanted to make sure he could get to the contents even if the generator went out. Good thinking.

All they had to do was guess the numbers and dial them. Mitch could take an electric keypad apart and figure it out in minutes. Very rarely had he seen an old-school strongbox like this before. On the two occasions he had, he'd blown off the door to get to the contents. That wasn't an option here.

"Any chance the CIA offers a safecracking class?" He looked at Megan.

She gave him a mysterious smile, lay on the floor and flattened her ear against the lock, then began to turn the dial slowly.

She was very handy on a mission, he had to give her that. She did a great job and looked good doing it. His gaze hesitated for a second on the way the moonlight outlined her curves.

She worked the lock while he moved back to the door to stand watch. Then finally she opened the safe, took out what looked like a ledger book and slipped it under her tank top where the elastic of the material kept it in place.

"Here." He helped her put the bookcase back in its place, then they were out of there.

He grabbed a granite statue on the way out, the bust of a famous South American revolutionary.

She tossed him a curious look.

He just flashed her a smile then headed for the room with the balcony.

They made it up to the roof without trouble. At the back of the building, Mitch aligned himself with the guard below. Held out the bust. Dropped it.

At the exact time when the heavy bust cracked the man's skull, Mitch let out a monkey screech to mask the noise. Then another to mask the sound of the guard folding to the ground.

He lowered himself down the side of the building, using window frames for support, jumping the last eight feet. He knew how to jump silently. Megan probably did, too, but he caught her anyway, just for the pleasure of being able to hold her in his arms.

Then they melted into the bushes together and headed for the building that held the explosives.

"I can't believe we have to go back in there again." She shuddered when they were at the hole that allowed entrance into the crawl space, a creepy, yawning mouth of darkness. No matter. He'd been in worse spots. "I'll go. You stay here and stand guard."

Her spine stiffened immediately. "I'm coming with you. You might need help in there."

He shook his head. "You always want to help everyone, but you don't want to take help from anyone. Is that an oldest sibling thing?"

She brushed by him so she'd be first in. "I don't know what you're talking about. I'm not like those helpless women you're used to, and if it makes you uncomfortable, I'm sorry."

He grinned as he followed her.

Other than *hot* and *trouble, helpless* and *clueless* had been the first two words that had sprung to mind when he'd first laid eyes on Megan Cassidy. About the last two adjectives, he'd been severely mistaken. About the first two, he'd been right on the money.

A low hiss cut through the quiet, freezing his limbs and sharply refocusing his thoughts. *Snake*.

He pulled his knife out inch by inch, avoiding any sudden moves. "Megan?"

"I've been bitten."

His breath hitched. He heard the sound of snake scales brushing against his boot, sliced down, hit flesh. He dropped the knife to light a match to see the damage. He'd cut the snake in half, but it was still trying to bite his boot. He speared the head with his knife, careful not to go too far and skewer his own toes.

The match went out. He lit another. Now that the damned snake wasn't moving, he could examine the markings.

"It's not poisonous." His heart began to beat again.

"It sure stings." She rubbed the side of her left hand against her leg.

"The bite is swelling."

Some antibiotic cream and allergy medication would be good, but their supplies were in their backpacks, at the barracks assigned to Juarez's men. They couldn't go back there. Their gear had to stay where it was.

No one would notice that the two of them were missing until morning. The men probably figured they were having some private fun in an out-of-the-way place. But if someone got up in the night and saw their gear missing, he would want to know where they'd gone off to.

Mitch had his most important possessions on his body: his gun and ammo, his knife and his canteen. He crawled another few feet then stopped. They had to be under the trapdoor. He reached up and brushed his hand against the wood planks, brushed off a couple of slimy slugs carefully so they wouldn't land on his head. A plank moved. There. The door.

He got in position and slowly pushed up the square piece of wood. "Stay here," he whispered. "Hold the bag. I'll hand down what we need."

At least she didn't argue about that.

He pulled himself up without a sound, crouched and listened. Couldn't hear anything, not even snoring. The light was on out in the main room of the building, a slim line of it coming through under the door. It wasn't really enough, but he didn't dare light a match in here, so he searched by feel, first looking for the right kind of boxes, then opening them and reaching inside. He handed down several sticks of dynamite before the eerie silence began to bother him, prickling his instincts.

He glanced at the door. Inched closer to it, pushing it lightly. What he saw stopped him dead in his tracks.

Somebody was lying against the door. Mitch couldn't hear the man breathing—he held his own breath to make sure he would catch the slightest sound. He pushed the door a little wider. The man fell over with a soft thud, into a pool of dark red liquid.

The single lightbulb that hung from the middle of the ceiling revealed another man on the floor near the table, lying at an unnatural angle. Other than that, the room was empty.

Mitch pulled back into the explosives room. "Come up here."

She handed him the bag first. "What's wrong?" She worked herself up, despite the fact that her left hand was now significantly swollen.

A good reminder that time was of the essence. "There are two men in here with their throats cut. I don't like it."

Then she was finally up and taking in the

bloody scene. "Cristobal really is making his move tonight."

"Somebody is doing something." He let his brain work on that while he looked through the stash of explosives.

Now that he had enough light, he could see that about half the boxes were empty, half held dynamite and a small special case hid plastic explosives. Disappointingly little, but he grabbed what was there. He shoved what he needed into the duffel bag he'd stolen earlier then swung it over his shoulder and moved through the main room, grabbing whatever else he could find that would be useful on their way home: an extra knife and gun for Billy, food, a bottle of tequila, more matches, a flashlight.

He handed the alcohol to Megan who sloshed some over her hand, disinfecting the puncture wound. It had to burn like hell, but she didn't even flinch. The alcohol would kill the germs and prevent infection. But she also needed something to counteract the allergic reaction she was having. Except there wasn't anything like that within easy reach. She would have to wait until they were in the jungle.

He reached the front door in a few more

steps, turned off the light, then opened the door an inch. He didn't see anyone out there. Might as well leave this way instead of through the crawl space again. In case the snake had family.

They made it out unseen, rounded the building, keeping close to the walls, and moving to the back so they'd be out of sight of whatever murderers roamed the compound tonight. When he looked back at Megan, he caught her flexing her left hand. The whole arm looked stiff.

They'd better hurry.

They moved forward carefully, watching every bush, every shadow, every stack of firewood to make sure nobody was lying in wait. But they didn't run into any resistance. The first man they saw was the guard in front of the Don's house, which was now completely dark. The guard now sat with his back to the wall, his head hanging back. He looked like he was sleeping. Only when they got close enough could they see the moonlight glinting off the blood at his cut throat.

The enemy was inside.

Megan looked at Mitch, her eyes wide. He swore under his breath.

All right. There was still a chance they

could do this. As long as they were alive, they had a chance, he thought, following Megan as she moved toward the main door which stood slightly ajar.

Cristobal's men would be upstairs. Their goal would be the Don's bedroom and office, Mitch reasoned. The path to the basement might still be clear.

He didn't get his wish.

Two men stood in the entry hall, guarding the bottom of the stairs. And just like that, the stealth portion of the mission was over. Mitch and Megan exchanged a glance.

He took the one to the left, Megan took the one on the right. One shot each to the head. Then they ran for the basement, locking the door behind them.

They heard boots slamming on the floor. Shouting. Men headed for the front door. Cristobal's men must have thought the shooters had pulled back outside. Good.

Mitch ignored the ruckus, stuck enough plastic explosives on the lock on Zak's cell to blow it. "Stand back."

Bang. The alarm didn't go off. Cristobal's men had probably cut the generator cords. He hadn't wanted to do that earlier, knowing the lights going out all of a sudden would alert the guards. But Cristobal had enough men to take out the guards before making his move on the house.

"You grab the kid," he told Megan and went for Billy.

He used the other half of what little plastic he'd found to blow that lock. *Bang.* The explosion busted the lock, all right, but the bottom of the metal door got twisted and stuck in the opening.

They had no time for this, dammit. Mitch kicked the door in. "Come on."

But Billy didn't move.

"Let's go." Mitch turned on the flashlight he'd requisitioned.

Billy sat on a blanket on the floor. His clothes had half rotted off him, his hair was matted to his head. His eyes were sunken and red-rimmed. "Malaria," he said with a shrug. "I told her not to come back. Don't waste time on me. You got the boss's book?"

Mitch nodded, trying to process what he saw. His heart sank.

Confirmation that they had the book put a little light back into Billy's eyes, even as more boots slammed upstairs. The house had to be full of Cristobal's men by now. And because of the explosions, they would know that something was going on in the basement.

Mitch glanced at the wall at the back of Billy's cell and placed the dynamite strategically at the bottom of the wall, hooking together the fuses, which were in sorry shape. They did have a rat problem in the compound. He twisted and tied together the frayed chunks as best as he could.

"Zak is ready at the bottom of the stairs." Megan was pushing into the cell. "Oh, God. Billy." She rushed to her brother's side.

"Take him out of here," Mitch ordered.

Megan was already pulling her brother up. She supported his weight, which couldn't have been much, and dragged him toward the door, her face set in a mask of hard resolve.

"Told you not to come back for me, sis. You never listen."

"There's a chopper on the roof. I'll get you home. They'll fix you up at the hospital."

Mitch whipped his head around to stare at Megan. She could fly a chopper? *Hot.* He grinned. It sure would make their way out of here easier.

"I'm too far gone," Billy said.

She ignored that and led him behind one of the cement pillars.

Mitch lit the fuse, then ran to join them. Zak was safe at the stairs. "Heads down!"

The fire raced about halfway up the fuse then went out. Damn the rats.

He ran forward, lit another match and tried again.

Again, the fire went out before it reached its target.

Cristobal's men were banging on the basement door, trying to break it down. Gunfire sounded above. That would take care of the lock in short order.

An explosion many times bigger than what Mitch had been able to achieve with the plastic shook the building from above, nearly knocking them off their feet.

"I'm guessing that would be the chopper," Billy said, his tone resigned. "Give me that." He snatched the box of matches out of Mitch's hand and limped forward.

"Billy, no." Megan moved after him.

Billy motioned her back. "You keep back. I know what I'm doing."

There was something in his eyes that made Mitch grab for Megan and yank her back. He wouldn't let her go.

"Fuse's worthless," Billy said as soon as he was close enough to see. He turned back, his gaze settling on Megan. "You get home safely. Tell Mom I love her. Amy, too. If things had gone differently...I wanted to marry her."

"Billy!" Megan lunged forward, nearly tearing Mitch's arm from its socket, but he held her tight.

Then Billy held the match to the end of one of the dynamite sticks directly. "I always hated the thought of dying slowly in a place like this."

Mitch threw himself on Megan who fought him like crazy.

"I'd much rather die like man," Billy told them.

And then the dynamite blew.

Megan screamed, a heartrending sound Mitch knew he wasn't going to forget as long as he lived.

The wall opened up, and Mitch could hear chunks of cement tumbling, although he could see little in the dust. He waited long enough to make sure more wouldn't fall on their heads, then grabbed Megan and Zak, pulling them both through the opening as the basement door burst open somewhere behind them. Bullets chased them all the way to the bushes.

They were all coughing, their eyes and throats filled with dust.

"To the hole in the fence." Mitch pointed the way.

Zak broke away and darted forward, saving his own skin. Megan pulled back. Mitch wouldn't let her go, but dragged her resolutely forward as bullets flew around them. He used his free hand to lay down some cover, shooting back.

The building behind them was engulfed in flames. The exploding chopper shaved off the top floor. Mitch's dynamite took out a good chunk of the basement. The place looked ready to collapse any second.

Megan beat on his back, screaming, "I can't leave him!"

"He's dead."

"I can't," she sobbed.

His heart broke for her, but he couldn't stop to comfort her. He broke into a run, dragging her along without giving her a chance to escape.

"He died so we could make it out of there. If you go back and they kill you, too, his sacrifice will have meant nothing," he said when they were through the hole and far enough that they could slow to catch their breaths.

Her eyes were glazed. She looked at him, but she didn't look like she heard what he said.

He stopped and shook her gently. "Once in your life, accept help! He wanted to do what he did. He was too far gone. He would have never made it out of the jungle. He gave us Don Pedro's book and our lives. His death meant something."

She went still then, at last. Nodded. He no longer had to hold her to keep her with him. When he started out again, she followed.

"I *will* bring these people down one day," she promised him as she wiped mud off her face, the mixture of dust and her tears.

He could hear Zak a dozen feet ahead, thrashing through the undergrowth.

Shots cut through the night. They were being followed.

Mitch shot a few rounds back that way as he broke into a run, with Megan close behind him, shooting like a banshee.

HER HEART WAS BROKEN. She felt as if a black hole had sucked her in. She functioned on reflex, but her mind was a wasteland of grief.

Men were still chasing them. That made no sense. Zak had meant something to Don Pedro, but he meant nothing to Cristobal.

Why would he waste men, sending them after Don Pedro's no-consequence prisoner?

"Why don't they quit?" she asked Mitch who half dragged Zak through the jungle. They'd caught up with him once his first burst of energy had run out.

"They must think we have something they want."

"Drugs?"

"I don't think so. There must be hundreds of pounds of that at the compound. They wouldn't risk life and limb in the jungle at night for another couple of bagfuls. They know we're on foot and can't carry much. I don't think it's the Don's playbook. How would Cristobal's men know we took it?"

"Then what?" She tried to see where she stepped, which was a hopeless business.

"What's the most important thing to Cristobal?"

"Power?"

"He wanted Don Pedro gone," Mitch agreed. "What if the Don wasn't in his room when they went for him?"

"Like he knew something was up and took off?"

"And Cristobal's men think he's with us." They had been following an animal path, but now Mitch darted into the thick of the jungle. He held out a hand for them to stop and get down behind him.

"Let them get ahead of us," he whispered. "We'll take them out from behind. Better us chasing them, then them chasing us."

He wanted the power position. She agreed. But her mind was still back at Don Pedro's place.

"We made a lot of noise. We broke out. They put two and two together," she whispered as she put it all together herself at last. It all made some very discouraging sense. "Why can't they let the Don go? They probably killed most of his men by now. They have his compound."

"Someone like Don Pedro could have other strongholds, other men. He rules a small army, scattered around the jungle, protecting his various businesses. Whoever wants to supplant him can't afford to let the man reach his support base."

A group of men ran past them down the path. Mitch waited a minute before he got up to go after them. Megan and Zak followed, trudging back onto the path that promised easier going. Only then did they realize that a second part of the group had lagged behind.

There were bad guys ahead of them and bad guys behind them. Mitch, Zak and Megan were sandwiched in the middle.

Part of her wanted to stop and stand her ground. Wanted to take the bastards out. She didn't care if she died here, too. Just now, she didn't care about anything.

Except then her mother would have to deal with the loss of two children. And her brothers would get it in their thick heads that they had to get revenge for her and Billy. And the last thing she wanted was to put any other member of her family in danger.

"Megan," Mitch whispered. "I know you're hurting, honey, but I need you to step out of it and commit to survival."

Honey?

"You're going to make it out of the jungle. You're going to survive this for Billy. I'm going to help you, and you're going to let me." He stepped closer to her, pressing his back to hers. "I take the back, you take the front." He even handed a gun to Zak who was pulling off the path, looking ready to run away. "You help Megan."

She set her feet slightly apart and braced her back against Mitch's. "All right."

Flashlights panned the jungle behind them;

she could see their beams from her peripheral vision, but she kept her gaze forward. She had to be ready to shoot at the first group once Mitch opened fire on the ones behind them.

The men shot first, and Mitch responded. Nearly every one of his bullets found their targets, judging by the shouts of pain that erupted in the night. The first group quickly turned around and backtracked, shooting at anything and everything. Zak panicked and returned fire long before they came into sight.

"Don't waste bullets!" Megan called to him, but he couldn't hear her in the din.

Megan held her fire until the men were within reach, until she knew she could do the most damage. Here they came. She squeezed the trigger over and over again.

The enemy fell.

She was numb, her finger fused to the trigger. Many died, but the ones left kept coming. They were close now. Really close.

Close enough to throw a hand grenade, she realized as a flash and bang blinded and deafened her, and the force of the explosion knocked her to the ground.

Chapter Thirteen

The grenade almost shook Mitch off his feet. He saw Megan go down and grabbed for her. Zak dove for the bushes, spraying everything behind him with bullets.

Their enemies had expected a lull in return fire after the grenade exploded, so they'd all come up from cover. Zak's wild spray of bullets had everyone scrambling back, which gave Mitch enough time to grab Megan and duck behind some trees.

Zak was still shooting. Panic had probably locked his muscles. Mitch joined in, firing at Cristobal's men until Megan had recovered enough to continue. And then they were off, on the move again, through the thick of the jungle where every step could be fatal.

Megan led, with Zak in the middle and Mitch bringing up the rear. They were all exhausted and injured to varying degrees. The wound on Mitch's leg that Megan had bandaged up ages ago didn't hurt too badly, but it did slow him down a little. And that was more than he could afford.

Zak was running out of steam fast. He wasn't used to this pace, and his broken jaw was clearly making him miserable. But of their combined injuries, Megan's snake-bitten hand bothered Mitch the most. The whole arm was swollen now, up to her shoulder. He'd seen it when the grenade had flashed.

He needed to find a native plant the forest people called corsh to make a poultice for her. The sap of the low-growing leafy weed helped allergic reactions and even neutralized mild poisons. If only they could stop. If only he could use the flashlight in his backpack to make the search easier. But he didn't dare use it. Light would give away their position.

THE FINAL BATTLE CAME at dawn. Everyone could see at last and that lifted their confidence. Both sides wanted to end the chase. Rapid fire was interspersed with short breaks while weapons were reloaded and men searched for better cover.

Some larger rocks, or any kind of cover would have been nice to protect them as they made their last stand, Mitch thought as he shot back and moved forward to look for a sustainable position. He burst out of the woods one step behind Megan, slowed as he took in the cliff in front of them. The drop to the bottom measured at least a hundred yards, the other side of the gorge about thirty yards away.

Not a distance they could tackle in one leap.

A Kapok tree had fallen across the canyon, or perhaps it had been cut that way on purpose to serve as a bridge. But that must have been a long time ago. Weather had rotted the wood. When Mitch kicked it, the spongy consistency didn't fill him with optimism.

The underside of the trunk that rested against the cliff had been hollowed by jungle critters or the elements, further weakening the structure, he realized as he looked more carefully.

He turned to the others. "We can't cross here."

"Now what?" Zak mumbled through his broken jaw, his eyes wide with fear. "We're gonna die in this stupid jungle, aren't we?"

"We'll have to make our last stand here." Cover or no cover. Their luck had run out.

Megan scanned the area, a grim expression on her face. She'd barely spoken since they'd left the compound. Her heart was broken, a dangerous condition for a soldier in battle. Her pain ripped through Mitch's gut. He wanted to talk to her, wanted to console her. But that would have to wait a little longer. Right now, they couldn't afford to take a single second to think about anything else but the fight. Cristobal's men had fallen back, but weren't far behind.

Mitch examined the terrain. If they couldn't find cover, some high ground would do, but there wasn't any of that, either. Except...

"Can you climb?" he asked the kid.

Zak shook his head, looking ready to drop from exhaustion. He was out of bullets, too. The kid wouldn't be much help. Mitch had to get him out of harm's way.

"Get into the hollow of this tree." Mitch bent and checked it for dangerous critters. They didn't need another snake bite.

Zak glanced at the space—large enough for him to hide in if he curled into the fetal position, which he did. "Can you see me?"

"You'll be fine as long as you keep quiet."

"Where do you want me?" Megan asked, leading the charge.

He hated to see her this dispirited. "We'll be up in the trees."

She immediately scanned the tallest ones and picked one for herself. He wished they could go up together so he could help her climb, but they'd be better off dividing the enemy. So he headed toward a tree several yards away. If all went well, the enemy would enter the clearing right between them.

Lianas helped his climb; a couple of nasty snakes slowed it. He dropped them on the trail below. With luck, they'd bite one of Cristobal's lackeys. He picked his position carefully, in the fork of a branch that provided protection from two sides. He hoped Megan had done the same. He could no longer see her. She'd done a good job of hiding in the foliage.

Megan was falling apart on the inside, but on the outside she was still a top-notch operator, taking care of business. Even seasoned soldiers couldn't always pull that off. His respect wasn't easily earned, but Megan had earned that and more. She had his loyalty. He would see her out of here in one piece or die trying.

He'd do the same for Zak. He'd done it for all the other men he'd rescued out of hot spots before, men whose lives had been put into his hands. Yet his devotion to Megan went deeper, to a level he wasn't altogether comfortable with.

If they survived the day, they were going to have to talk about where they stood. He wasn't sure if he should be pleased or scared. All he knew was that his insides were tied up in knots every time he thought about any harm coming to her.

Endless minutes ticked by. Then the noises of the jungle changed suddenly. Birdcalls turned shrill and warned of new danger. People were coming.

For a second, Megan pulled from cover, making her face visible to him, but not to anyone below. They didn't say anything. Her beautiful face looked tough yet vulnerable.

He was falling in love with her.

And then one of Cristobal's men came into view. Mitch aimed, fired and took him out. Judging from the way the bushes moved and the force of the returning fire, there were at least twenty others behind him.

How in the hell? Cristobal must have sent fresh men in the night who'd followed the sound of gunfire and had caught up.

Twenty against two.

Those weren't the best odds, but Mitch was

who he was, and Megan was who she was, and they made a hell of a team.

He neutralized two more men before a bullet nicked his heel. Good thing he wasn't Achilles. Aside from the burning pain, the injury didn't much interfere with the business of taking these goons out.

Megan got her men, one by one, with enviable precision. Each shot was a kill. Her brother was not forgotten, nor would he ever be. She was fueled in equal parts by stone-cold professionalism and red hot revenge, a deadly combination.

The enemy saw the danger, too, and blanketed her position with fire.

If she was hit, she didn't cry out.

He tried to see how many men were left down below. They'd gotten a bunch of them, but there were still a dozen men shooting from behind cover. They had limitless ammunition and plenty of practice at shooting monkeys out of trees. The branches around Mitch were riddled with bullets. He figured Megan's hiding spot had to look the same.

One of the men below them was going to get lucky sooner or later. The only way to survive a battle against these odds was to finish it quickly.

A bullet grazed his knee. It got just close enough to rip his pants and take off some skin. Mitch took out the shooter, and the man next to him. That one had a radio clipped to his belt. Good, now the bastard wasn't going anywhere with it. They were going to need that later.

He kept on shooting at every leaf that moved. Megan didn't take a break, either. Then more bullets flew at them, and the next thing he knew, she was falling out of the tree.

His heart stopped. The ground was too far away, the fall unsurvivable.

"Megan!"

Somehow she caught herself on a branch, her boot wedged between two tree limbs. She hung upside down, gun still in hand, blood covering the side of her neck and face.

He went a little crazy then, sliding down on a liana, not caring that he was falling too fast or that the bark of the plant took the skin off his palm. He squeezed off one bullet after another all the way down, a war cry tearing from his lips.

When his boots touched the ground, he barely felt his busted heel. He plowed forward, like a robot, men falling before him. Blood ran on the jungle floor. He, too, was covered in it. This small patch of jungle looked like a slaughterhouse when he was finished.

And all that time, all he could think of was Megan.

The gun had fallen from her hand. She hung listlessly from the branches, held only by her boot. If her small foot slipped from it...

He climbed the tree faster than he ever thought possible. "Megan! Megan, honey?"

She shook her head. Focused her eyes. They narrowed immediately as she squeezed off a shot, and when he twisted, he saw a man he'd missed earlier. The last of Cristobal's foot soldiers fell with weapon in hand and a disappointed look on his face.

Then Mitch was there, pulling Megan up and cradling her in his arms. The bullet that had knocked her out of the tree had cracked her collarbone. Mitch found two more bullet holes in her chest. He yanked up her tank top and gave thanks to God. Don Pedro's game book had acted as a bulletproof vest, saving her.

A last gift from Billy, who'd told them about the book in the first place.

"Hang in there." He made a pressure bandage, took both of their belts off and tied her to his back with them, then carried her down the tree.

"Is it over?" Zak stumbled their way to investigate the silence. "I'm hungry." He finally spotted Megan who'd passed out from blood loss on the way down. "She doesn't look good."

"Shut up and go find the man who had a radio. We need it," Mitch snarled at him. "And get me a boot. Right foot. About this size." He showed the busted boot on his foot. Blood seeped through the hole.

He ignored that and checked Megan's wound first. The bullet was still lodged inside her, in a way that actually prevented more serious bleeding, so he decided to leave it in. When he got her to a hospital, the doctors could deal with it. And he *would* get her to help.

He grabbed his canteen and washed the blood from her face.

Her eyes fluttered open after a moment. "What happened?"

"You got shot. Stay still." He offered her water, and she drank.

"Is it bad?" Her eyes were glazed with pain.

"Nope. You'll live to boss me around another day. Try to move as little as you can."

He limped off into the undergrowth, and didn't come back until he found what he was looking for. Corsh weed for her swollen arm, and some small brown berries that had disinfectant qualities for her brand-new bullet wound.

He treated her injuries then ripped two strips off the bottom of his T-shirt and bandaged her. Man, he hated to see her in this shape. "I wish we could rest."

She looked offended. "Have you ever seen me take a nap in the middle of the day?"

He smiled at her. He loved her, there was no way around it.

Fat lot of good it did for either of them. The situation was impossible. With the kind of jobs they had, they'd never see each other. But nobody ever said love was convenient. From all accounts, it was a major pain. He felt it.

He looked over at Zak who was checking the dead. Beyond the jaw that couldn't be helped until they got to a doctor, the kid had no other visible injuries. So Mitch took a few minutes to deal with his own cuts and abrasions, and his heel.

"Need any help?" she offered.

She could be half dead, and she'd still be the one who wanted to take care of everybody.

He shook his head. "Don't worry. I'll live to annoy you another day."

She reached out and took his hand, her amber gaze locking with his. "I'm getting used to it. You're not always that annoying."

He squeezed her fingers. Never wanted to let her go. "I have my good days, huh?"

"Good minutes." A ghost of a smile crossed her face. "Let's not get carried away."

"Why not? I think you should get carried away." He bent over and picked her up. Took a few steps to see if he could walk without putting too much weight on his heel. He set her back down again when Zak returned with an armload of loot.

"You're not carrying me." Her eyes narrowed as she laid down the law.

"You've lost too much blood."

"Are you calling me a wimp?"

Zak dumped his bounty at Mitch's feet: a couple of pieces of beef jerky that the kid looked at mournfully since he couldn't chew, ammunition, a boot that looked like it would fit, a shortwave radio. "The rest of the stuff is covered in blood. I'm not touching it."

"This is more than enough. You did good. Let's get ready to move."

"We have a radio. Call in the cavalry," the kid argued with him, forming the words painfully.

"We have to get to a spot where a chopper can land," Megan educated him.

Mitch turned on the radio, dialed a channel he knew U.S. military in the region monitored, then sent a coded message that gave their rough location. He added a special code so the Colonel would be alerted. Then he turned the thing off. No sense in running down the battery.

"I'll be carrying her." He shot Megan a look. "She's got a broken collarbone, and she's lost too much blood."

"I'm hurt, too," the kid protested.

"I'm not carrying you, so you'll just have to live with it. Grab that bag and let's get going."

"My jaw is broken."

"I never said you had to carry the bag with your teeth." Zak was a poster child for tough love. He needed some, and Mitch wasn't about to coddle him. He started out heading northeast along the gorge, looking for a way across.

In the end, they didn't need to cross. They found a flat rock ten miles down the way big enough for a chopper to land. He made another call on the radio and kept transmitting so the rescue team could track the signal to their exact location. Then they had nothing to do but wait.

Dusk was gathering by the time the extraction team arrived. The sound of the helicopter's rotors reached them from the distance. Mitch tossed some wet leaves on the fire he'd started and sent the thick smoke upward, fanning it with a palm leaf. Soon the chopper came into view above the trees, and he kicked the fire apart, so the smoke wouldn't be an impediment to landing.

He didn't know the men who jumped out to help them aboard. They weren't from his team. The Colonel must have requested assistance from whatever military unit was close and available.

"Thanks. I appreciate your help." It felt odd to be on the other end of a rescue. He wasn't used to it.

The rescue team knew better than to ask

any questions that didn't have to do with their physical well-being.

A medic had ridden along with the chopper. Zak demanded drugs until he was knocked out completely. Megan refused them.

"You need to go to a hospital, ma'am," the medic told her as he left her side to talk to the pilot.

They'd strapped her to a stretcher to keep her broken collarbone from moving. Mitch sat next to her and took her hand.

She closed her eyes. Her face was drawn. He had no trouble guessing the path of her thoughts. She was thinking about Billy. She had sworn not to leave the jungle without him, had planned on him being with her when she headed out of here.

He squeezed her fingers. "Your brother would be proud of you."

"I failed." Even her voice sounded broken.

"Don Pedro's game book has enough intel to clean up half the jungle. Because of Billy, and because you came for him, you'll set back the drug and gun business at least a decade. This will save thousands of lives. Tens of thousands. This is why Billy took on the job."

She nodded. Then she opened her amber eyes and looked at him. "I love you."

He stared at her as she closed her eyes again. He loved her, too, but he was not the man she needed. He could be lost on any mission, just like her brother. No way would he risk putting her through that pain. He couldn't stand the thought of her suffering like this because of him.

Minutes passed while he looked at her, bewildered. His feelings switched back and forth between elation and despair. By the time he gathered himself, she'd fallen asleep from the combination of blood loss and exhaustion.

She slept the whole three-hour chopper ride to a small rural hospital. Medical personnel were waiting to examine her and Zak. Mitch, too, but since the Colonel was also there waiting for him, he decided he could do the debriefing before they started poking at his heel.

"I'll come back as soon as I can," he told Megan before marching off with the Colonel.

But an hour later, he couldn't find her. The CIA took care of their own, it seemed. They'd sent someone for her, and she'd already been taken away, back to the States.

Chapter Fourteen

Hopeville, Pennsylvania, three months later

Mitch sat in the small apartment he'd rented as a home base in between missions, and looked at the printouts of a spacious condo the Realtor had done her best to talk him into buying. He'd gotten the reward money for getting Zak out of the jungle in one piece. The little twerp was fine. And now he was thinking about starting up a business that taught jungle survival.

A nerve jumped in Mitch's eyes every time he thought of the kid.

At first, he'd refused the reward money. Then the Colonel had stepped in, told him he was going to accept it because he had worked for every penny of it, and that was an order.

He didn't want the money. He didn't much want the condo, either. He wanted Megan.

Not searching her out was a daily battle.

But in the end, he loved her enough to do what was best for her. He wasn't it.

Hell of a thing. He was pretty sure she was the best thing that could ever happen to him.

Funny how fate could mess up so badly.

Since he'd last seen her, he'd been on another mission and back. His heel was as good as new. His heart was in tatters.

He'd almost messed up this last job. He was losing his focus.

He needed to talk to her, he decided. So he couldn't talk himself out of it again, he grabbed his cell phone and called the Colonel.

"I need a leave of absence, sir. For personal reasons."

"Everything all right?"

"Fine, sir. It's time to visit some old friends. You wouldn't know where Jamie Cassidy hangs out these days?"

"I wasn't aware you two were close friends. You never did an op together."

"No, sir." He wasn't about to elaborate.

A moment of silence passed. "Why don't you come into my office to sign the paperwork for that leave. I'll dig out his file."

"Thank you, sir."

Now he would have to do it. Now he was committed. When he got back from his leave, the Colonel would expect a full report on Jamie and how he was recovering.

Mitch ran his fingers through his hair. If he happened to see Megan while he visited Jamie…

He stood up and headed for the door, caught himself at the last second and glanced down, wincing at the state of his clothing. Brooding home alone all week didn't do much for a person's image. The Colonel would chew him out if he saw him like this.

He padded up the stairs. He could afford enough time for a shower. He added a shave, too. If the Colonel thought something was wrong with him, the man would get on his case and insist on answers. Mitch didn't have any of those.

All he knew was that he was in love with Megan Cassidy and a relationship between them was impossible. A solution was brewing in the back of his head. But it was probably too drastic. He needed to speak to her before he made any big life changes. Leaving the SDDU wasn't a move he entertained lightly. But he would do it for her, if she thought she could accept him.

He reached the base an hour and a half

later. The Colonel's secretary announced his arrival.

"Colonel." He stopped in his tracks when he realized the Colonel already had a visitor. A man about Mitch's age sat in a wheelchair. He had amber eyes and blondish hair in a familiar shade.

"Jamie Cassidy. Mitch Mendoza." The Colonel made the introductions. "Jamie stopped in to discuss something with me this morning. He wanted to see you, too."

They sized each other up. Jamie's handshake had plenty of steel in it.

"You were there when my brother died," he said in a tone void of emotion. But his eyes held tempered steel.

Oh, hell. If Jamie Cassidy blamed him for Billy's death, then Megan probably did, too. "Billy was too far gone to make it out. He died a hero's death."

"That's what my sister says," Jamie allowed, but his countenance didn't soften any.

Mitch's heart drummed faster. "Is she here?"

The Colonel answered that. "She's in the next room, going over your report of the op to see if she can add anything. I asked for her help. The materials you two brought back are of some significance. Further ops are being planned."

The words *I want in* were on the tip of Mitch's tongue, but he couldn't say them, not until he talked to Megan, not until his future was decided.

"Sir?" He glanced toward the door.

The Colonel nodded. "Go ahead, soldier."

Jamie scowled at him. He wasn't as sure about what had gone down at Don Pedro's as Megan was, apparently. Either that, or he resented Mitch asking about his sister. The man knew the life, what the unit meant, the kind of work they did. He probably would have been happier if none of his teammates met Megan at all.

Mitch understood that, even agreed. But he couldn't help himself when it came to Megan Cassidy.

He walked down the hall and knocked on the door the secretary pointed to.

"Come in."

Just hearing her voice made his heart beat faster.

She looked exactly the same as the first time they'd met. The no-nonsense ponytail was gone, and long, blond waves tumbled down to cover the scar on her neck. She had on a smattering of makeup she didn't need. Her flirty dress ended an inch above her knees. He swallowed as he stared. He'd never seen her in a dress.

Wow. All right. Okay.

She looked elegant and poised, too beautiful to behold. Way out of his league. What had he been thinking? If she blamed him... Hell, he blamed himself half the time. He'd spent a couple of sleepless nights thinking about what he could have done differently.

Almost as many nights as he'd spent thinking of her, with him, and nothing else but tangled sheets.

She glanced up from the stack of papers she'd been reading.

"Mitch!" She flew to him and wrapped her arms around him.

She smelled like some exotic jungle flower.

He'd thought she'd give him a cool reception, so he was stunned by the entirely different welcome. For a second, he couldn't respond.

She pulled away, a shadow coming into her eyes. Took a step back, a more businesslike look settling onto her face. "They're putting together an op to go back in the jungle. Are you going?"

"No."

She looked disappointed. "I am."

"A joint mission with the CIA?"

"I begged the Colonel to put me on the team. With Jamie's help."

His head was spinning. "I'm quitting the team."

"Why would you do that?"

"Because I want to marry you and I never want to see you in the kind of pain I saw when you lost your brother."

Her amber eyes went wide. "You're trying to guarantee that you won't die on me?"

Now that she put it that way, it sure sounded stupid.

"I'm buying a house. A condo, actually." Maybe that would help. "I'm trying to—"

"You want to marry me?" Her eyes narrowed. "When we were in the chopper and I said I loved you, you didn't say anything back."

"I needed a little time to recover. I needed to figure out a way I could make our relationship work."

"And your way is to quit?"

That did sound bad. He wasn't a quitter. A woman like Megan wouldn't want a quitter for a husband.

"Do you want to quit?" she asked.

"No. But I can live with it," he tried to explain. "I can't live without you."

"You won't have to. I'm going with you."

"Where?"

She looked at him as if he was slow in the head. "Back to the jungle. I'm coming over to Colonel Wilson's team in six months."

"You can't." He wasn't sure he could handle seeing her getting shot again.

"Watch me." She was all cold steel on the inside. And all hot curves on the outside. A combination that would keep him fascinated for the rest of his life. Then a thought popped into his head and stole his breath. "Why wait six months?"

His gaze fell to her midriff. How much could a man trust an old condom he found on the bottom of a drug dealer's duffel bag?

Her belly was flat, but you could never tell. His heart jumped up into his throat. Spots swum in front of his eyes.

She pulled a folder from her bag on the floor and handed it to him.

His hands shook as he opened it, expecting ultrasound pictures. He blinked hard when he saw the photo of a familiar one-year-old instead. *Cindy.* The world spun with him.

"What are you doing with my sister's file?"

"Finding her."

He couldn't allow his hopes to rise. That part of his heart was dead, even if Megan had awakened the rest. "I spent years chasing down every lead. I searched hard. There was nothing to find."

"But have you ever searched with all the tools of the CIA at your full disposal?" she asked.

"And you're giving them to me for the next six months?" Hell, with something like that, he could do miracles.

"For the next six months. That's when the Colonel is shipping a team back to the jungle. He'll need that long to process all the information we brought in and devise a strategy."

Of course she would. But she wasn't going without him. No way.

"We'll do this together." Because when the chips were down, the truth was he'd rather have her at his back than anyone else he knew. "And when we come back we get married?"

"Jeez, don't be so pushy." But she grinned. "Maybe."

His heart leaped.

"And while we're waiting for that deployment, we'll find your sister. I'm going to do everything in my power to help." She smiled at him.

He stepped closer. "I love you, you know that."

When she stepped into his arms, he wrapped himself around her. Kissed her with all the need of the three long months they'd been apart. He was never going to let her go again. There wasn't another like her on the planet.

She pressed against him, smiled against his lips as she brushed against his hardness. His body was more than ready for her.

"And what might that be?" She teased him between kisses.

"I'm very happy to see you."

"It's either that or you had a run in with a banana spider." She laughed at him, then jumped and wrapped her legs around his waist.

He caught her, got lost in her. *She was his.* He didn't deserve her, but as long as God saw it fit in His generosity to bring the two of them together, he would do whatever it took to make her happy and keep her safe.

He didn't know how long they'd been kissing when someone cleared his throat behind them. They jumped apart, suddenly mindful of where they were.

"There are rules about fraternization in the SDDU rule book, soldiers," the Colonel said with a hard voice. But his eyes were dancing with mirth.

"The SDDU has no rule book, sir," Mitch retorted as the tips of his ears turned red.

"Impertinent, the lot of them." The Colonel turned to Jamie who was right behind him. "Are you sure you want to rejoin a team like this?"

"Yes, sir."

"Jamie, you can't be serious." Megan ran to him, crouching next to the wheelchair and searching her brother's face.

"This man has more experience than any ten others put together," the Colonel told them in a no-nonsense tone. "He'll be an operations coordinator at our Texas office."

Mitch wrinkled his forehead. "We don't have a Texas office."

"It's on a need to know basis. We started up operations in South Texas six months ago. Too many of our international ops uncover terror plots with links to sleeper cells and the like in the U.S. We needed to add another office here. Texas Headquarters will investigate drug and gun smuggling as well as human trafficking from Central and South America as it relates to suspected terror activity."

"If it's top secret…" The puzzle pieces were falling into place in Mitch's mind.

"You're being transferred there effective immediately. Megan will begin working there when she starts with us in six months," the Colonel responded. "You are both experts on South American ops."

"Jamie?" Megan still sounded unsure, but a change was slowly coming over her. It seemed she was beginning to understand that this was exactly what her brother needed to get his life back on track.

The Colonel knew, Mitch thought. The Colonel knew and he saw to it. No wonder his men would walk through fire for him.

"There are still things I can contribute." The harsh lines softened on Jamie's face. "I can coordinate missions and play wedding coordinator at the same time. I'm good at multitasking. From the looks of you two when we walked in, the sooner we hold that wedding, the better."

"She hasn't said yes, yet," Mitch put in, just to make sure Jamie knew he'd asked. Jamie

Cassidy wasn't a man he wanted to tangle with, wheelchair or no wheelchair.

All eyes moved to her.

The Colonel raised an eyebrow. "My soldiers are not known for being wishy-washy."

"Megan?" Jamie watched her closely.

"Oh, please. I'm too old for peer pressure."

Nobody blinked.

"Seriously." She patted an errant lock of hair into place at her temple, looking flustered suddenly. "He doesn't need me for *anything*. He made that plenty clear, every day we were together."

Was she serious? Mitch stared at her.

Did he want to say this with two other guys in the room? He didn't have a choice.

He went down on one knee. "Megan Cassidy. I need you more than air. Please help end my misery by staying in my life. Because without you it's not worth living."

She cocked her head, and looked like she was struggling to suppress a grin. "So you're asking for my help? Just to be clear."

"I'm asking."

"And you will let me save your life if the occasion should arise, and will admit you need such assistance freely."

"Yes."

"Hmm."

"Is that a yes?"

A smile of pure joy broke loose all over her face as she plowed into him and nearly knocked him over, locking her arms around his neck and kissing him. "Yes." Then she kept on with the kissing.

He kissed her back hard, then remembered the others. But when he looked behind him, the Colonel and Jamie were gone, the door closed.

His body came alive with need for her. His heart opened fully, for the first time in years. "I love you, and I need you."

"I love you and I need you, too." She slid her hand under his shirt.

He choked back a laugh. "Here?"

"It's a lifesaving op." She backed toward the desk. "Think of it as an emergency."

Certainly felt like it. Heat flooded him as he slipped his hands to her hips.

"So who's saving who this time?" He asked as he eased her dress up her lean thighs.

"We're saving each other," she said as she kissed him.

* * * * *